Midnight

Mhairi O'Reilly

Copyright © 2024 Mhairi O'Reilly

Kindle Edition
Paperback
Hardcover

Written by Mhairi O'Reilly
All rights reserved. No part of this publication may be
reproduced, distributed or transmitted in any form or
by any
means, or stored in a database or retrieval system,
without the
prior written permission of the publisher.

Disclaimer: The material in this book is for mature
audiences
only and contains graphic content. It is intended only
for
those aged 18 and older.

This book is a work of fiction. Any names, places,
characters,
or incidents are a figment of the author's imagination.
Any
resemblance to persons living or dead or actual
events is
purely coincidental

"The moon is full, the night is deep,
nature is alive—the only thing missing
is you, next to me as we sleep."
Nicholas Staniszewski

1

Prologue
I collapsed back in the faded lawn chair with a huff, my eyes fixed on the crackling fire as I took a long swig from my chilled beer. I had been at the South Carolina clubhouse for a week, and the restlessness inside me seemed even more intense than when I arrived. Thoughts of Aislynn flooded my mind, and I forced myself to shut them down. I knew better than to entertain them because Aislynn's love for Leather was plain to see, and I didn't stand a ghost of a chance.

Plus, the part of me that should have been hurting right now—*my heart*—wasn't, it was still beating the same as always, so was it love?

Yet something about her drew her to me, this burning need to smooth away her rough past and make her world brighter. But I had to face the truth. I wasn't the man to banish her demons and needed to move on.

"You look lost, brother," Bolt said, his gravelly voice drifting from the chair beside me as he raked a hand through his auburn hair. Bolt was this club's Sergeant at Arms and had become a friend over the past few years whenever club business brought me through.

I gave a half-hearted shrug, eyes still glued to the fire's hypnotic dance. "Not lost, just restless."

"Well, you know the cure for that," Bolt said with a wink, pointing to Taylor, an extremely curvy blonde gyrating provocatively to the throbbing rock music, casting flirtatious glances our way. "She'll wear you out good, but fair warning, she's a screamer."

I chuckled, "Yeah, I noticed. Thought someone had let an injured wolf in last night." I pondered a moment before asking, "You know any good places around here to explore after dark?" I loved the mystery of nighttime, the velvety darkness, the muted sounds, the peace it brought.

Bolt considered, then answered, "There's a waterfall deep in Old Man's Forest, though it's a bit of a hike, and remote, found it when I was a teenager."

"Perfect," I answered, listening to his vague directions before strolling to my bike, throwing a leg over the powerful machine, and riding off into the dark night.

The clubhouse soon faded into the distance, the sound of laughter and rock music replaced by the low purr of my bike and the whispering of the wind. The moon hung full in the sky, throwing a silvery sheen as I slowed down, turning onto the narrow dirt road barely bigger than my bike, the underbrush crowding in on all sides, a tangle of leaves and vines brushing against my arms and legs. I stopped and dismounted when the road ran out, leaving my bike parked by a gnarled ash tree.

My heart sped up with excitement as I navigated deeper into Old Man's Forest on foot. My body came alive with anticipation of the unknown.

The night was alive with a myriad of sounds—hoots from a distant owl, the scuttle of unseen critters in the undergrowth, and an occasional rustle that implied something larger lurked in the mysterious shadows. But the deeper I ventured, the more tranquil it became until it was just me and my thoughts buzzing in the quiet that only happened at night.

Ahead, I could just make out the faint rumblings of water cascading over rocks. The sound grew louder as I moved forward, echoing through the dense forest like a lullaby whispered by the trees themselves. A clearing came into view ahead and it was bathed in moonlight, nestled among the trees where a modest waterfall cascaded—its beauty lying in its pure simplicity the same as the one on my property.

Moonlight danced on the water's surface, casting an array of glimmers and sparkles.

But was my vision playing tricks on me?

There, at the edge of the cascade, was a small woman, her body swaying rhythmically as she gazed up at the starlit sky.

Her silhouette was striking against the glow of the moon, her loose, flowing hair glinting like pouring flames. Her bare feet seemed to barely touch the ground as she danced with a delicate grace that belonged to the fairies and nymphs of the old legends, the ones my Papu used to tell me about on our hikes through the woods when I was a kid.

My breath hitched in my throat as she slowly turned my way. Despite the distance separating us, I could see her eyes—two blue jewels sparkling with vibrant life.

Who was she?

A sense of unreality washed over me, briefly making me question whether I was dreaming. But there she was, real as ever—her presence illuminated vividly by the moonlight. I should leave and quit creeping in the shadows like a stalker.

But then she pulled her dress over her head, throwing it to the ground.

For a moment, all I could do was stare, awestruck by the pale beauty of her naked body touched by silver moonlight. She moved closer to the waterfall and my heart pounded in my chest; I was trespassing in an intimate moment, invading her privacy, but my fascination and my hardening cock wouldn't let my feet move.

She reached out to touch the flowing water, letting the cool droplets splash over her fingers. A laugh bubbled up from her throat, echoing musically through the clearing. It was a pure and unrestrained sound that sent a thrill straight to my cock. The tension I carried since leaving West Virginia dissipated, replaced by my captivation with a red-headed wood nymph.

I sensed him immediately, his presence pricking my skin as if the air itself vibrated with his existence. For a week now, I had come to this secluded sanctuary, drawn by its primal magnificence. Here, surrounded by nature's raw splendor, I could shed my controlled life that choked me and allow me to find peace by being surrounded by what I loved.

At first, his sudden appearance unnerved me, sending a shiver walking down my spine. But instinctively, I knew he posed no threat. And tucked away in my bag lay reassurance—a small handgun, cold and ready. So, I turned to him with cautious curiosity and found him in the moonlight and my breath hitched, damn he was gorgeous. His dark eyes ensnared me, their scorching intensity reaching across the small meadow that separated us.

Desire blazed through me like wildfire, leaving me craving experiences beyond the gilded cage of my unwanted sheltered life. Tonight, I felt reckless, eager to explore the unspoken connection where it led. The certainty that my family was about to destroy any chance of such temptation only strengthened my resolve.

Yes, it was dangerous, but I had little left to lose.

Giddy anticipation bubbled up as I dipped my fingers into the cool silk of the water, a thrilling sensation coursing through my body at my daring as I pulled my dress over my head, throwing it to the ground. A laugh spilled from my lips as I gave myself up to the freedom of this moon-kissed oasis and jumped into the pool of water and when I came up, my eyes found him once more. "Come join me," I called with a playful wave, and the bold invitation hung tantalizing in the air between us.

I didn't know how he would respond, but an inexplicable sense told me we were fated to meet here. Without hesitation, he moved toward me, deliberate yet graceful, his eyes burning into mine. My breath snared in my throat, stunned by the raw magnetism that radiated from him.

He was even more good looking up close.

For an instant I felt self-conscious in his presence, acutely aware of my own unremarkable features, the bright red hair and freckles, my petite curves. But I shook off the uncertainty, for his eyes reflected all I needed to know. He desired me, and my skin was on fire despite the chill of the water.

He stood at the water's edge, his eyes burning into me as he shed his black vest and shirt, revealing a torso rippling with tattooed muscle that gleamed in the moonlight's glow. With casual elegance belying his powerful physique, he stripped off his boots and jeans, standing proud and bare before me.

My eyes widened at the sight of his erect cock, and when I felt the blush spread over my face, I prayed the shadows would hide it, but when my eyes found his once again, his smirk proved that prayer went unanswered.

The water rippled around him as he entered, electricity charging the serene night. He moved with virile grace, parting the water with powerful strokes. Our eyes stayed locked, the outside world fading away until it was just us two—drawn together by forces that seemed beyond our control.

He reached me in a few long strides, his commanding presence tempered by gentleness. I watched a smile tease his lips, releasing butterflies to flutter wildly in my stomach. In the moonlight, his chiseled features and smoldering eyes exuded raw passion.

"Are you sure?" he asked, his voice a sensuous caress.

I nodded, words trapped between my pounding heart and dry throat. Our gazes locked, sharing unspoken words of what we both wanted to happen. He brushed back a wet lock of hair, his touch igniting sparks down my body—an electrifying sensation beyond anything I'd known.

"Yes," I whispered, my breath fluttering against his skin. Our eyes searched and questioned without speaking the words aloud.

His fingers traced my face, trailing down my neck until his hand rested over my frantic heart. It pounded against his touch, mirroring his own racing pulse. "Are you afraid?" he murmured, his voice husky. His question hung in the hushed night. Underneath my façade of courage lurked a fine tremor—not of him, but of the unknown.

"I'm not afraid," I answered steadily, surprised by my conviction. The fear remained, but exhilaration, an intoxicating rush that made me feel truly alive, eclipsed it. His tranquil presence dissolved the last of my doubts, opening me to a new awareness that pulsed deep in my core.

His eyes softened, offering unspoken reassurance, and as he drew me closer, I felt the heat rolling off his skin in waves. His hands framed my face as he leaned down, his breath warm on my lips—a silent request in the night.

I met his intense gaze unflinchingly, granting consent with my eyes. A smile ghosted his lips before he erased the distance between us. The velvet brush of his mouth on mine ignited a wildfire that blazed through my veins. His kiss began softly yet quickly deepened, coaxing me into returning his hunger with my own.

His arms enfolded me, pressing my body to his until all I felt was him—his breath, his heart, his heat. An overwhelming sense of belonging suffused me, so powerful, and I felt complete in his embrace—like I found my home.

Suddenly he broke the kiss and gazed at me with such need it stole my breath away. "What's your name?" he whispered against my flushed skin.

I had to swallow before I could coax the words from my throat. "Hadleigh," I murmured, my voice barely louder than the whispering breeze that rustled through the surrounding trees. A shiver of anticipation ran through my body as he repeated my name, rolling the syllables over his tongue as if savoring them.

"Hadleigh," he said again, slightly louder this time. The sound of my name spoken in his velvety tone was so intoxicating that a hot flush spread across my cheeks, but I didn't look away. There was a pause filled with heavy silence before he finally revealed his own name. "I'm Kaven."

The name suited him—it was strong and unique.

I let it dance on my tongue until his lips once again took mine, his arms pulling me flush against his body.

I've never been so fucking turned on in my life. My body was literally on fire with the need to touch her, kiss her, be inside her. I still believed that just maybe I had passed out and was having one hell of a hot dream.

But no dream could create this richness of sensation—the softness of her skin against mine, the sweet taste of her lips, the intoxicating smell of her. All my senses were alert like never before, drunk by her presence. I was so fucking lost in her and I sure as hell didn't want it to end.

The moon bathed us in silvery light as we moved together in the water. Her arms draped around my neck, pulling me closer still. Every inch of me ached to be closer to her, to know her on a level deeper than just physical. It felt like gravity itself was pulling us towards each other, an irresistible force that neither of us could refuse, and I wasn't about to fight it.

Fuck no, this feeling was too fucking good.

As we continued to kiss, our hands explored every inch of each other's bodies, our movements making the water ripple around us. Hadleigh ran her fingers through my hair, pulling me closer as I groaned into the kiss. My hands traveled down her spine before cupping her ass tightly, pulling her against my hard cock.

She gasped at the feeling, her legs wrapping around my waist instinctively. I lifted her effortlessly, carrying her towards the nearby blanket she had spread earlier. As I laid her down on the soft fabric, she arched her back invitingly.

"Fuck, you're so beautiful," I whispered hoarsely against her neck. My lips and rough jaw trailed hot kisses along her collarbone as my hands roamed freely over her body once more.

Her touch ignited sparks down my spine—an electrifying sensation beyond anything I'd ever known. She whimpered softly as the feel of my calloused fingertips tracing circles around one of her nipples, making it harden under my lustful eyes. "More," she breathed out, arching into my touch even further.

I complied without hesitation, my warm breath fanned across her erect nipple before I took it deep into my mouth, sucking hard on it as my tongue swirled around it teasingly. She cried out loudly this time, throwing her head back in pure pleasure as I worked my magic on her breasts.

I couldn't get enough of the sound of her moans filling the night air. It only fueled my need for more—more of her body, more of her voice, more of everything. I moved lower, kissing and nibbling my way down to her thighs.

I looked up at Hadleigh from where I kneeled between her spread legs and nearly lost control at the sight that greeted me. Her glistening pussy was the most beautiful pussy I had ever laid eyes on, and I had the experience to back it up. Fuck, I wanted a taste, but I would come before my cock experienced heaven.

So, I positioned myself at her entrance, rubbing against it teasingly before pushing inside in one smooth motion that left us both gasping for air once again.

Holy fuck, she was tight and hot around me; it felt like heaven slipping into hell and back again within seconds flat as I thrust in and out of the woman who held me captive within just a small time together under the moonlit skies. This was such a strange magical night we would forever remember as ours alone. The feeling of being so deeply connected with someone else on such an intimate level was overwhelming, but so fucking addictive.

Our hips moved in perfect rhythm with each other as if they were one being sharing this incredible moment together... our hot lovemaking knew no bounds as we rode out our mutual desire for one another. I never wanted it to end, but I couldn't hold out any longer and when I heard her cry of release, felt her tighten around me, it was over for me with a loud growl as I held myself inside Hadleigh, my cock unwilling to leave. We collapsed together, spent yet satisfied beyond words.

As our bodies trembled in unison, she clung to me, her fingers digging into the hard muscles of my back. I gasped for breath, my heart pounding against hers as the aftershocks of our shared orgasm coursed through me, our breath ragged pants, our bodies smeared in sweat and lust.

I cradled her closer to my chest, interlacing my fingers with hers. My heartbeat finally slowing, the sounds of the night lulling us into drowsiness. With my other hand, I traced lazy circles on her bare shoulders, tracing the freckles that dotted her skin, adding to the powerful sense of tranquility.

But then three things hit me at once and sent a sudden jolt of realization that sent an icy shock through me: One: this was the most erotic experience of my life, two: Hadleigh was a virgin and three: I hadn't used protection, something I had never done in my life, but tonight I had got carried up in the moment.

Breaking the silence, I whispered her name, "Hadleigh." It felt like a confession as I entwined my fingers deeper into hers.

She stirred against me, half-asleep and content. Her eyes fluttered open, capturing the moonlight and reflecting it back at me. As she felt the tension in my body, one eyebrow arched questioningly. "Kaven?" Her voice was a sleepy murmur, lost in the blanket of serenity that had wrapped itself around us.

Running a hand through my already tousled hair, I tried to keep my voice steady as I confessed my sin. "Hadleigh... I just realized... we didn't use any protection."

I watched as my words seemed to take a moment to register in her clouded mind. Then slowly, the drowsiness vanished from her eyes and was replaced with a wide-eyed surprise.

Hadleigh

Oh, no, no, no, my mind chanted at his confession. The truth struck like lightning—sudden, blinding, an electrifying realization of the dare I had taken, stepping boldly into my first experience on my own terms. Would I change it if I could?

Never.

Most girls lament their first time, but mine? It was ecstasy, a rush of pure pleasure and intoxicating freedom that left me desperate for more. I was already craving another plunge into the addictive bliss Kaven had gifted me.

Kaven's face was lined with worry, his handsome features twisted with concern. Seeing him troubled like this, knowing it was my doing, twisted a knot in my gut. I had to ease his fears, to lift the heavy burden clouding his brow. With a calm resolve, I locked eyes with him, my expression neutral, my lie carefully hidden.

"It's okay, I'm on the pill for my periods," I assured him, my voice steady despite the racing beat of my heart. It was deception born out of necessity, an attempt to ease his fears and reassure him that everything would be alright. Deep down, though, worry clawed at the edges of my conscience, reminding me of the consequences that could follow such a fabrication.

Relief swept across his face like a soothing tide, erasing the creases of worry. His body relaxed, a visible release of tension. "And I'm clean, Hadleigh, I swear it... and you... you were a..." His voice faltered, tangled in a web of curiosity and hesitation. He cleared his throat, visibly unsettled, grappling with the weight of his unvoiced thoughts.

Heat flushed my cheeks as embarrassment and vulnerability

clashed inside me. I squirmed, struggling under the intensity of his gaze. "Yeah," I whispered back, barely audible. "Does it matter?"

The silence that followed was thick with uncertainty, the unspoken words hanging heavily in the air between us. I could sense his hesitation, his struggle to find the right words. It was as if he was tiptoeing through a minefield of emotions, careful not to trigger an explosion that could shatter the newfound connection we had forged.

Finally, he spoke, his voice low and steady. "No, not at all," he assured me. "I just didn't expect it and you didn't act..." His sentence trailed off again, leaving the thought unfinished. He swallowed hard; the nervous energy was palpable. "It's a good thing, and what we experienced was fucking incredible."

His eyes searched mine, probing for a truth only half revealed. "What in the hell are you doing out here at night... *alone?*"

I nestled deeper into his embrace, the warmth of his body a comforting shield against the chill of the night. A playful smile tugged at my lips. "I discovered this spot last week while hiking. It seemed magical, and it truly is, and meeting you here tonight proves it. There's nothing to fear in the night that isn't there in the daylight."

Interest flickered in his eyes, a spark of curiosity. "So, do you live around here?"

I shook my head, weaving another strand in my web of half-truths. "No, I'm here for two weeks on a post-college graduation trip with a friend," I explained, allowing the moment of escape to envelop me.

"College? What did you study?" His interest was genuine, his tone eager.

A laugh escaped me, light and free. "Nothing thrilling, I promise. I have a degree in botany."

Surprise raised his eyebrows, his gaze intensifying with admiration. "From the way you were dancing, I would have guessed something artistic. Botany must be real interesting."

Laughter bubbled up from inside me at the memories conjured in my mind. I looked up into his eyes, a hint of nostalgia coloring my voice. "Years of childhood ballet, and yes, to me botany is fascinating," I confessed. "But enough about me. What brings you out here and in the middle of the night?"

This thing with Hadleigh—it began as mutual lust, an electrifying attraction, a fantasy that I expected to fizzle into awkwardness afterward. But lying here with her, it wasn't like that at all. The more she spoke, the more fascinated I became. She was unlike any woman I'd ever met; sprawled on this blanket under the stars, she captivated me completely.

"I'm around this area for a bit, love exploring at night, and this spot came recommended," I shared, trying to keep the mood light. "But my buddy never mentioned I'd encounter a beautiful wood fairy dancing in the moonlight."

A playful smile lit her face, her freckles dancing across her nose and cheeks. "My family can be overwhelming," she confessed, "so I steal away to places like this, where I can just be me."

I understood, but what she gave me tonight—her trust, her virginity—was a special gift. Curiosity got the better of me. "Why me, though?"

She paused, her expression pensive. "It's hard to articulate. There was just this gut feeling that you were the right person... sounds bizarre, I know. You must think I'm odd."

Her refined speech hinted at a privileged upbringing, but her demeanor was anything but snobby, like most rich people I'd encountered. "My mama used to say that the right person appears and takes you by surprise," I murmured, pulling her a bit closer. "Doesn't make you strange at all to feel that way."

Suddenly, a buzzing from her bag sliced through the quiet, and Hadleigh scrambled to retrieve her phone. Checking it, she bit her lip. "I need to go—I didn't realize how late it was."

Midnight

She began to dress hastily, and I followed suit, my thoughts whirling with the need to see her again. "Will you be here tomorrow night?" I asked, the urgency clear in my voice.

Her eyes sparkled as she tied her damp hair up. "Yeah, I'll be here," she promised, her smile infectious.

As we trekked back to the dirt road, her familiarity with the path was obvious, confirming she'd been there often. At the road, I eyed my bike and asked with genuine curiosity, "How did you get here? You couldn't have walked—it's miles from town."

With a mischievous grin, she moved behind the tree where my bike was parked and wheeled out a Venom Ghost chopper. "It's no Harley, but it gets me where I need to go," she chuckled, securing her green helmet.

I laughed, astonished and fucking utterly charmed by her. "Tomorrow night, yeah?" I said, swinging onto my bike.

"Tomorrow night," she confirmed, firing up her engine. With a last wave, she cruised down the narrow dirt road.

Left there with a goofy grin plastered on my face, I kicked my Harley to life and followed her, already anticipating what tomorrow night would bring.

Easing off the throttle, I guided my motorcycle into the cavernous parking garage. The sound of the engine reverberated off the cold concrete walls, amplifying my racing heart. I hastily stashed my helmet in the compartment; my cousin Lizzie's text still fresh in my mind. It was nearly three in the morning, and I had to return before the night guard at our vacation villa switched shifts. A family getaway, meant to celebrate mine and Lizzie's graduation, but had unwittingly become a cover for another one of my secret escapes.

Adrenaline fueled my steps as I sprinted the two blocks back to our villa. As I neared its wrought-iron gate, I slowed to a stealthy creep. Darting through the narrow opening in the gate, I edged along the side of the house. My heart pounded a relentless rhythm in my ears as I peeked inside and exhaled in relief. Roberto, our night guard, was still lost to his snores. His secret was safe with me; his slumber had been my ticket to my nightly adventures.

With catlike caution, I tiptoed past Roberto and up the stairs, slipping into my room unnoticed. No sooner had I closed the door than the light snapped on abruptly. Lizzie stood there, arms crossed over her chest, her face covered with worry and disapproval.

"Hadleigh," she chastised, "you promised you'd be back hours ago. What you're doing is reckless."

Lizzie and I were polar opposites in every way except age. She was all dark hair and piercing green eyes, a tall figure sculpted by discipline and grace. Meanwhile, I embodied our grandfather's wild red hair and freckles and an untamed spirit who loved nature more than people.

"You won't believe what happened tonight," I enthused, flopping down next to her on the bed. The thrill of my recent encounter still electrified my senses. "I met someone..."

"Hadleigh..." Lizzie frowned, her tone laced with confusion and concern. "I thought you went to the waterfall?"

"I did," I confirmed, a wicked smile playing on my lips. "And he's the most gorgeous man I've ever seen... it felt like destiny."

"Hadleigh, please don't tell me you..."

My nonchalant shrug was deliberately ambiguous. Her sigh was heavy with resignation. "Hadleigh, don't forget your obligations. You're betrothed to Samuel Flavio."

The mention of Samuel—a man as frigid as his power and amassed fortune—made me wince. "I know, but this guy, Kaven... there's something about him that feels right, like we were meant to meet and I'm just tasting freedom before I'm chained to that unbearable man."

"Just remember your limits," Lizzie cautioned, her voice filled with worry.

As I retreated to the bathroom, thoughts of Kaven consumed me. The ghost of his touch still lingered on my skin, his scent tempting me to forgo the shower. This dangerous game I was playing thrilled and terrified me in equal measure—a high-stakes gamble where my heart was on the line, and I could suffer major consequences of my actions.

"Where you off to?" Bolt asked from his barstool as I navigated my way through the crowded clubhouse common room.

Smiling, I moved to his side, responding, "I'm heading back to the waterfall."

Bolt sniffed the air, and a sly grin crept onto his face. "Showering and dousing yourself in cologne for a simple hike?"

I shot him a playful smirk. "You never know when you might encounter a wood nymph under a waterfall."

Bolt's grin broadened as he playfully punched my shoulder. "You met a chick in the fucking wilderness!"

"The best night of my life," I admitted with sincerity.

Bolt chuckled. "Are there any places women don't fall at your feet? You're one lucky bastard."

I shrugged nonchalantly. "Catch you later, Brother." My anticipation of seeing Hadleigh again was making me impatient. Thoughts of her had consumed me since we parted, my mind and body craving her presence.

Mounting my bike, I set off towards the waterfall. Upon arrival, I found Hadleigh's bike parked by a tree. Her early arrival sparked a tinge of uncertainty—could last night's magic be recaptured? Would the same attraction be there, or would things be awkward? As I stepped into the clearing, that doubt evaporated.

There she was, already in the water. My gaze followed her as she played and a spark of pure lust ignited inside me, the same as last night. There was just something about this woman that did it for me in a fucking big way.

My pulse raced, just like my bike's engine, as she moved closer to the cascade, the silver droplets falling onto her naked body. Her breasts were bathed in moonlight, their peaks hardened from the cold and enticingly visible. I felt the unspoken invitation stirring in the air.

Obeying a primal instinct, I stripped off my clothes, my heart pounding in anticipation. Unencumbered by leather and cloth, I could feel the cool forest breeze against my skin. The sight of her was stirring something deep inside me—an animalistic urge that was both scary and intoxicating as fuck.

As I approached her cautiously from behind, my hand moved to touch the smoothness of her back, which seemed to shimmer under the soft glow of the night's full moon. A soft moan escaped her lips as I ran my fingers up her spine, sending shivers down mine.

Her body responded to mine instinctively, pressing back into me. The sensation of our bodies pressed together was electric. With every breath we took, I could feel our chests rising and falling in harmony—her excitement amplifying mine.

I cupped one breast, teasing a sensitive nipple between my thumb and forefinger while my other hand gently trailed its way down her abdomen. Her quiet gasp was all the encouragement I needed, my fingers dipping lower to explore her warmth, a finger slipping into the wetness of her pussy.

She turned slightly so she could face me; our eyes met in a gaze as intense as it was intimate. Slowly but surely, those lovely hips began to grind against mine—slow rhythmic circles that matched the rhythm of our beating hearts.

The waterfall roared nearby, but her heavy breathing drowned everything else out in my ear, the telltale signs of pleasure etched on her face. Our bodies moved together as one; savoring each wave of pleasure as it washed over us.

My cock slipped effortlessly into her, deeper and deeper, until every inch of me was enveloped in her warm pussy. Her muscles clenched around me, urging me towards an almost excruciating feeling of euphoria.

Each thrust sent ripples of pure pleasure through my cock, making it throb to the point of pain. The sounds of our pleasure grew louder and louder, drowning out the hum of the night and the roar of the waterfall. Finally, with a long-drawn-out cry, she surrendered, and I followed with a bellow, as we surrendered to the waves of our orgasms crashing over us.

Floating in the afterglow, entwined in the water, reality seemed to fade away outside this enchanted clearing. Feeling her shiver against me, I whispered into her damp hair, "Let's get out of the water."

Guiding her towards the shore, we found solace in the warmth of each other's bodies; I took the side of the blanket and gently draped it around her, a simple act that brought a smile to her face.

Settled on the blanket under the moonlight, we basked in the shared silence. She traced invisible patterns on my bare chest with her fingertips while I played with her damp hair. We needed no words to fill the quiet intimacy between us.

After a bit, I propped myself on one elbow, looking down into her beautiful face. "Tell me something about you, Haddie," I said, breaking the silence.

A soft laugh escaped her lips before she spoke. "Haddie?"

"Hadleigh is a mouthful," I explained with a chuckle.

A soft smile crossed her face as she answered my question. "My favorite color is dark purple, much like the color of your eyes right now."

I prompted for more. "What else? Something unexpected."

She thought for a moment before replying, "I hate marshmallows. Always have."

This made me laugh, a rich, warm sound that echoed through the trees. "You can't be serious. I thought everyone loved them."

She shook her head, her nose scrunching up adorably and was sexy as fuck for some reason. "Not me. Can't stand them."

"Now you tell me something about Kaven," she prodded, running a finger down my chest that made my dick twitch to life. I had the feeling she was changing the subject, so I let her and figured I'd circle back.

We spent the rest of our time together talking and making love, connecting in a way that I knew my life was about the change deep in my soul, the way my papu used to warn me about.

The intoxicating power I held over this man was a heady addiction, one I wasn't sure I could ever abandon. Five nights we'd met, each encounter escalating in intensity and wild abandon. Now as our eyes locked, my lips and tongue teasing him with a slow torment, I questioned how I could ever exist without this connection, without him.

His fingers wove through my hair, pressing gently against my scalp as I welcomed him into my mouth. His voice, rough with desire, rang in my ears. "Haddie," he rasped, "take me deeper." *And so I did.* Even as tears welled in my eyes and breathlessness threatened to overcome me, I never broke our gaze.

The previous night had revealed Kaven's deep-seated desire for eye contact during our most intimate moments. The sight of his dark eyes clouding over with burning lust made me feel like the most enticing woman alive. His hand maintained a steady hold on my head as his hips began to move rhythmically, turning the act into something more primal that left me aching for more.

"Get ready, Haddie," he growled in warning. His grip on my hair tightened momentarily as he found his release, the sudden rush momentarily overwhelming me. As Kaven gradually released his hold, he carefully guided my head onto his thigh to recover. Looking up at him, I found his head thrown back in pleasure, his breaths coming out in ragged pants.

"Haddie," he murmured softly. His eyes slowly fluttered open to meet mine once again. "You're gonna kill me."

His words sent shivers of pleasure rippling through my entire body. I pushed away from his thigh, rising to my knees and reaching up, tracing a gentle finger along the line of his jaw. Our eyes locked once more; twin orbs of need reflecting off one another. "I only want to breathe life into you, Kaven," I breathed back a reply, my throat raw yet determined.

He reached up then, his hand wrapping gently around my wrist, pulling it down to press a simple kiss into the palm of my hand. "Then you're succeeding," he murmured against my skin, his hot breath tingling across the flesh. His lips turned upwards in an impish grin. "A strange method of resuscitation, but real fucking effective."

"Kaven, I'm leaving in two days," I declared, my voice dropping to a grave tone. "I'll miss you, miss this place so much."

"Do you really have to go? You're an adult, you can make your own decisions," he urged, his piercing gaze digging into mine. "We don't have to end this."

But he couldn't possibly understand the complications of my life. I had kept my family and past hidden from him during our time together. "It's not that simple," I murmured, resting my head on his chest.

"Well then, maybe I'll have to make you stay," he declared, a spark of determination igniting in his gaze as he pressed me beneath him, his eyes fixated on me. "I'll breathe fire for what we have into your veins until you can't even think about leaving." My response could only manifest as a sigh, surrendering to his passionate kisses trailing down my body. And with each hot kiss and sensual touch, I felt myself falling deeper into Kaven's spell.

At that moment, I knew that walking away from him would be impossible. I was falling deeply in love with him, willing to risk everything for a chance of happiness. Tomorrow night, I would reveal the truth about my family and pray that he would stand by me and find a way for us to be together.

Hadleigh

My heart hammered against my ribs as I slipped into the shadow-draped house. The silence instead of snoring an unsettling observation of Roberto's absence from his usual post. Anxiety clawed at my insides, yet a flicker of hope urged me forward. With cautious steps, I nudged the bedroom door open and slipped through the crack—only for the harsh glare of the overhead light to snatch away the darkness.

Mother stood in the center of the room, her arms folded like steel traps, her expression a turbulent storm of anger and disapproval. I froze, caught.

"Whatever you've been up to ends tonight," she declared, her voice slicing through the tension.

"I'm enjoying life, Mother—like any normal person would!" I retorted, my voice crackling with weariness. The chains of a predetermined fate were suffocating.

Mother's eyes narrowed, her finger jabbing the air toward me. "We've indulged your whims, Hadleigh. Allowed you your little escapade of becoming a botanist, roaming the woods like a common vagrant. But it ends now. You have duties that cannot be ignored."

"Why must I always be the one to sacrifice everything? Why not Lizzie? She's better suited for this life." Desperation crept into my voice. "I don't want to marry Samuel Flavio."

A sigh escaped her, then a look of sudden realization dawned on her face. "You've fallen in love with someone, you foolish girl."

"Can't I talk to Grandfather? Maybe he'll understand how I feel," I pleaded, my voice tinged with desperate hope.

Mother's laughter was bitter and hollow. "Do you want your lover to die?"

"Die?" The word echoed in my mind, a chilling tremor.

"Listen to me," she said, her tone solemn, her eyes piercing mine. "If your grandfather learns of this man, he will have him killed to preserve your engagement. His honor, his word, they are his bond—he will not risk them for your heart's whims."

The reality that she was right crashed over me like a wave. The men in our family, bound by blood and old codes, didn't play games. Kaven, the man who had quickly become my heart, was in danger because of me. When Mother commanded, "Pack your bags, we're going home," I knew it was an order I couldn't refuse, the grim reality of my life taking hold of me.

With a heavy heart, I began to pack, each item feeling like a stone in the burial of my dreams.

All day, my thoughts circled around Haddie like ants to sugar, each loop tighter, more urgent.

Did I love her?

My heart roared an undeniable yes, despite only knowing her for a short time. My brother Fenix had been right when he advised me that my feelings for Aislynn were a misguided attempt to atone for my sister Kezia's death, as if by saving Aislynn, I could rewrite the past. Did I care for Aislynn? Yes, but with Haddie it was different. With her, it was primal, fucking wild—an untamed connection that seared through my soul.

My Mama's words replayed in my mind, speaking of a spirit mate, that there is one person destined to intertwine with your essence, completing the puzzle of your existence. That was my Haddie, I knew it as sure as I was breathing.

Tonight, I resolved to peel back the layers of mystery she kept hidden about her life, ready to plead with her to stay or, if it came to it, to follow her wherever she might go, until I convince her to stay with me. But I just couldn't leave her and what we started together.

I leaned my bike against the familiar tree near our meeting spot, noticing her spot hauntingly empty. Haddie was always here before me, her seductive challenges a thrilling prelude to our encounters. Tonight, I expected no less, eager to discover what she had planned.

However, as I settled by the waterfall, the only sounds were the murmurs of water and the rustle of leaves, a music of nature that filled the growing silence. Minutes stretched into hours, and the moon climbed higher. But Haddie didn't appear. I waited, hope mingling with dread, tonight and then again the next night.

But Haddie had vanished, like a ghost whisked away by the wind, leaving no trace, not even a whisper of goodbye.

2

Two months later:

In the shadowed corner of the clubhouse, Valley grumbled disapprovingly, "You used to be a real riot, man." We were holed up in the wilder side room, watching the usual shit unfold. I'd ducked out of the main room to avoid Leather and Player, who had been eyeing me like a target since I rolled back in a few months ago. Leather's possessive jealousy over Aislynn was a ticking time bomb, and I knew better than to get caught in the crossfire.

Even a mere glance in Aislynn's direction would ignite trouble. It didn't matter that I no longer harbored any romantic interest in her. Leather was one jealous son of a bitch, always ready to ignite like a fuse, so I kept my distance. What really sucked was I still cared about her and wanted her to be happy and well, but I couldn't even ask her how she was doing without getting my ass kicked.

"Yeah, babe, he's got a point," Bunny chimed in, encircling me with her arms from behind and planting kisses on my neck.

I shrugged her off more forcefully than intended. "Cut it out, Bunny. Not in the mood. Go bother someone else." Ever since Haddie left, nothing felt right. She had left an indescribable void that no one else could fill, and here I was, snapping at everyone because bitterness consumed me and that wasn't like me at all.

She hadn't even said goodbye. Why should her ghost continue to hold me down? But here I sat doing exactly that, letting the memory of her chain me.

Stung by my reaction, Bunny retreated. Valley leaned closer, concern crossing his rugged face. "Hey, brother, we've been inseparable for as long as I can remember, and I've never seen you like this. Are you still hung up on that chick from South Carolina?"

"Drop it," I muttered, my gaze drifting over the room, forcing myself to watch the two sweet butts dancing naked on the pole in the middle of the room. Feel something dammit! I demanded of my cock, but nothing, not even a fucking twitch of interest. Haddie held a hold over me that I couldn't shake no matter how hard I tried. My dick only wanted her and what she could make me feel.

"This chick must have been something else to cock block without even being around," he chuckled, having been watching me. "You're really starting to worry me; you know that, right?"

"I'm fine. All I need is some time to get over it."

Valley smirked, mischief glimmering in his eyes. "You know what they say, don't you? The best way to get over old pussy is to dive into some new pussy."

"Nah, I'm swearing off women for a while. It seems like I always end up on the losing end," I replied, rising from my seat. "I'm outta here."

Valley simply shook his head, taking a long pull from his beer as he watched me leave. He didn't push further; he knew me better than that. We had been tight since childhood. He was the reason I found myself in the club instead of chasing bounties like my brothers. His old man had paved the way for both of us.

I stomped past the row of bikes parked outside; each one gleaming under the faint moonlight like silent beasts waiting for a wild ride. The night air slapped my face, sobering up some of the frustration simmering inside me. I fired up my Harley; the roar slicing through the quiet like a scream in an empty church.

As I peeled out of the parking lot, the cool wind cut through my jacket, but it couldn't chill the heat raging in my chest. The road stretched ahead, dark and inviting. Right now, it was the only thing that made sense.

I didn't head towards any particular destination. It was just me, the bike, and the endless night. Every mile I put between me and the clubhouse should have shed the heavy cloak it felt like I was wearing, yet the weight of Haddie's memory clung stubbornly.

A part of me wished I could just ride until the road ran out. Maybe somewhere along this endless black ribbon, I'd find a way to leave behind the woman haunting me. Maybe I'd come back differently, or maybe I wouldn't come back at all.

I stared at the man I was being forced to marry, my gaze filled with an indescribable mix of disgust and resentment. Samuel Flavio, with his icy demeanor that could rival the fiercest arctic storm, seemed completely unfazed by my emotions. All that mattered to him was the damnable contract that bound our families together.

After enduring another grueling dinner—one of many since our engagement was announced—we stepped out onto the patio, where my grandfather proposed a walk. "Samuel, why don't you accompany

Hadleigh for a walk in the garden? She has a remarkable talent for plants and such," my grandfather suggested with a glimmer of hope in his eyes.

"I would love to," Samuel's response was a lie impeccably disguised beneath a straight face. Taking my arm, he guided me down the stairs, his grip firm as I kept my hands clasped in front of me. But as soon as we were out of sight from the prying eyes on the patio, I jerked away from him, unable to suppress my mounting frustration any longer.

"I can't believe you won't put an end to this madness!" I snapped, my voice tinged with anger. "You don't even like me, and after what I confessed to you the other night..." My words trailed off. I had confessed my love for someone else, and the possible consequences of that love, hoping he would see reason, taking pity on me and end this marriage, but he refused to care because he was just a cold block of ice.

"For once, could you cease this incessant whining?" Samuel retorted, running his hand through his dark locks in exasperation.

"Whining?" I seethed, my voice dripping with disdain. "I'm being forced into a loveless marriage with someone who is harboring another woman in his penthouse, hidden away from the world."

His eyes hardened as he demanded, "How do you know about her?"

"I know many things, dear Samuel," I replied icily, feeling a surge of defiance within me. "And if you don't extricate us from this charade, I will make sure you and that woman suffer just as much as I do." It was a hollow threat, born out of my desperation and loneliness without Kaven, the man I loved so much, and missed with my very being. A dangerous move indeed, because Samuel was a powerful Mafia Boss, and I was walking on thin ice mouthing off like this.

In a swift motion, Samuel grabbed me by the arm, his grip tightening like a vise. "Listen to me, little girl," he snarled, his voice laced with a chilling intensity. "Never threaten me, ever. And never mention or attempt to approach Hope. You will regret it."

"How splendid," I retorted, yanking myself free from his grasp. "You're more protective of your mistress than your own fiancée. But let me assure you, Samuel, your threats hold no power over me. My grandfather would never allow you to harm me physically. So, keep your empty words. I am not afraid." With those defiant words, I pushed past him and fled into the garden, seeking solace in my sanctuary — the greenhouse.

I settled onto the swing nestled amidst my beloved plants, allowing myself a moment to regain composure. With each swing, my heartbeat gradually slowed, and my mind cleared. I desperately hoped that I could somehow convince Samuel to release me from this suffocating contract. He was the only one with the power to do so, yet my previous attempts had failed miserably. In this world, where women held no sway or influence, I should have known better.

Running away seemed to be my only option left, but the question loomed: where would I go and who could I turn to? I didn't know Kaven's last name or his place of residence; all I knew was that he belonged to some club, as he wore a vest bearing its emblem. However, he never left it on long enough for me to decipher any meaningful details. Furthermore, without help, I would never get far. But who could I trust enough to risk their neck for me? The danger was too great.

My hand instinctively drifted to my stomach, a silent confirmation of the truth I already knew. I was pregnant, carrying the child of a man I would likely never see again, except through the reflection in our child's eyes. The weight of that realization bore down on me, tears streaming down my face in an overwhelming wave of sorrow.

What was I going to do?

3

The sudden crash of my feet hitting the floor ripped me out of my dreams, and I came up swinging, fists aimed at whoever dared disturb me. "Ease up, tiger," Fenix laughed, effortlessly dodging my half-asleep punches. His smirk was wide as he loomed over me. "You planning on making this a regular crash pad?"

I slumped back onto the couch, rubbing the sleep from my eyes. The ride last night had been long, and my brother's place was a hell of a lot closer than the clubhouse. "Do you care?" I shot back, already knowing the answer.

"Not unless you cockblock some hot night I might have had going on," he shot back with a grin that told me he was half-serious. "If I had a lady planned, you'd have ruined one hell of a good time."

I snorted. "Bullshit. You wouldn't risk Mama catching her perfect son with his pants down."

Fenix shrugged, playing along. "Maybe I'm just picky about who shares my sheets. Not everyone's as indiscriminate as you." He'd be surprised to know I hadn't shared my sheets in months, not since Haddie.

Before I could rib him further, the door banged open and Bo stumbled in, still walking like he was made of old creaky parts. "What's this? Do I have to start locking my doors now?" Fenix grumbled.

"Saw Kaven's bike out front," Bo grunted, his voice tight. "Figured this was the first place to look."

The tension in the room spiked as Bo's gaze fixed on me. "How's Sarah doing?" he asked, though it sounded more like an accusation.

"She's fine, so drop it," I snapped back, irritation flaring. "She and Mikie are taken care of, better than you're thinking."

"In a damn biker clubhouse?" Bo's voice rose, anger clear on his face. "That's no place for a kid, or a woman you claim to love." I got my brothers didn't approve of me being in the club, but they didn't understand the brotherhood, thought it was all one big party and walking the edges of the law.

I stood, feeling my own anger bubble up. "Let it go, Bo. They're happy, and that's what counts."

Bo leveled a stern finger at me. "Watch it, kid. I might be busted up, but I can still take you down a peg. Now, let's grab some breakfast. Mama's expecting us."

Fenix laughed, "Kid? He's been taller than you since he was sixteen, old man."

"Yeah, but that doesn't make him stronger," Bo shot back, the tension draining out of him now that we were joking once more.

"Give me a sec," I said, pushing off toward the bathroom. I checked my watch—yeah, time for breakfast before church. Patch had me on call today, must be up for a run. But first, food. Mama's cooking was not something to miss, not ever.

Emerging refreshed, I found Fenix and Bo in a deep conversation about one of Fenix's old flames.

"Selena was something else. Remember some of the crazy shit she used to do?" Fenix asked with a wistful sigh.

"I remember her right hook," Bo replied, and they both laughed.

Grabbing my jacket off the hook near the door, I rolled my eyes at their reminiscing. "Are we going or what?"

"Don't worry, little bro, Mama won't start without us," Fenix said, his face splitting into another grin as he followed me out the door. Bo shook his head, but was chuckling as we left, the earlier tension forgotten.

When we reached her apartment, she was waiting at the door, her face creased in a smile that could outshine the sun. "About time you three showed up," she scolded lightly as we walked through the door, though her warm smile betrayed her feigned annoyance. We each received a hug before being ushered into the homey kitchen, where an array of breakfast goodies awaited us.

Stepping into Mama's kitchen felt like stepping into another world. Warm smells of cooking filled every corner and instantly cheered me up. What would someone like Haddie think of how simply we lived? I shook off those thoughts as I pulled a chair out at the long dining table.

As we settled down at the table filled with mouth-watering biscuits, fluffy scrambled eggs, crispy bacon strips and steaming mugs of coffee, Fenix kicked off another conversation and we laughed and talked about random shit as we ate. After breakfast, we all helped clear up under Mama's watchful eye before heading off toward our respective lives.

"I'll see you boys later," Mama said as we were leaving, hugging each of us tightly in turn. Her eyes lingered on mine a little longer than usual, her concern clear in her warm eyes. I gave her a reassuring smile in return before stepping out into the hallway, she always managed to know when something was wrong with one of her boys.

Outside, I revved up my bike and headed back to the clubhouse, hoping that Patch had a run for me. It would get me out of the clubhouse and take my mind off Haddie.

4

Hadleigh

Time was slipping away like sand through my fingers, and my desperation grew with each passing moment. This Saturday, I would be walking down the aisle, trapped in a gown that felt more like a shroud. As I stepped out of the dress shop and into the car, the last fitting of my wedding dress clung to me, a tangible reminder of the unwanted future looming over me. The very air seemed to thicken with dread, suffocating my hopes and dreams.

"Snap out of it, Hadleigh," my mother hissed, her voice a sharp whisper meant only for my ears. Despite her discretion, the driver glanced at us briefly in the rearview mirror. His name was Micheal, and there was no point in whispering. He knew the intricate web of our household's dramas.

I couldn't contain my frustration. "So, I'm supposed to smile and dance while being shackled into this nightmare?" I retorted, the bitterness in my voice sharp.

My mother exhaled, a sound heavy with both impatience and a weary resignation. "Don't think of it like you're being forced into it," she began, her hand reaching for mine as if to anchor me to this grim reality. "It's about the life it brings—wealth, influence, lineage."

"And what about love?" The word hung between us, fragile and forlorn.

With a scoff, my mother replied, "Love? A child's fairy tale. Men are faithful only until the next pretty young thing catches their eye. Even your precious lover would turn his back on you for someone else. Believe me, I've seen enough to know that love is nothing more than a lure used by men to trap you."

The image of Kaven, possibly with someone else, twisted in my stomach like a knife. He had every reason to move on; after all, I vanished from his life without a word.

"Hadleigh," my mother continued, her tone softening but her words cutting deeper, "perhaps it was a mistake to let you believe you could lead a different life, to let you dream so freely. I thought a taste of freedom might sweeten what was to come. But this—this is our world, our duty. No amount of dreaming can alter that."

"Why not Lizzie then? If it's just about alliances?" I shot back, desperate for any escape.

"Because you are the favorite, the mirror image of your grandfather in both looks and spirit. To him, this marriage is not a sentence but a crowning gift, entrusting you to the most powerful man he knows. He believes it's an act of love."

I slumped back against the leather seat, resigned. My mother, bound so tightly to these archaic ideals, couldn't see beyond the gilded cage.

As we arrived home, Samuel Flavio's imposing SUV greeted us. "Behave like the lady you are meant to be, Hadleigh," my mother cautioned as we stepped out of the car.

Inside, we learned Samuel awaited us on the patio. My heart sank further, but my curiosity peaked. Samuel never spent time with me that wasn't planned out by our families, and as he rose to greet us, I eyed him suspiciously. "I thought I'd take Hadleigh out for lunch," he announced unexpectedly, a tight smile playing on his lips. What was this sudden change?

"Oh, of course," my mother replied, nudging me with a look that brooked no argument.

Masking my distaste for him with a practiced smile, more curious than anything, I agreed. "Yes, I'd love to."

What was Samuel up to? And could this unexpected outing offer a glimpse of hope, or was it just wishful thinking, and this was only another link in my chains?

Hadleigh

In the secluded corner of the upscale restaurant Velvet Vine that he owned, the silence between Samuel and me stretched like an insurmountable chasm. The plush velvet booth embraced us, but its comfort seemed meaningless under the weight of our unspoken tension. With each clink of the silverware, the atmosphere grew more suffocating, a testament to the gravity of our situation.

Samuel's icy gaze met mine, his silence during the ride a foreboding message: "We'll talk at the restaurant." No further explanation, just that tantalizing promise hanging in the air, leaving me simmering with frustration and curiosity.

Unable to contain my mounting impatience any longer, I finally broke the silence. "Why drag me here if you're just going to sit in silence?" My voice carried a sharp edge, slicing through the quiet like a knife.

His response was a low mutter, his jaw clenched with determination. "God, I hope this works."

"What did you say?" I demanded, leaning in closer, desperate to catch every word.

"Listen, Hadleigh," he began, his voice dripping with urgency. His eyes locked onto mine with an intensity that made my heart race. "Neither of us wants this marriage, but breaking off our contract could ignite a war between our families." He paused, allowing the weight of his words to sink in. "But I think I've found a way out—a plan so risky it must stay between us. Do you understand? No one else can know."

"A way out?" Hope flickered in my chest, mingling with the adrenaline coursing through my veins.

"Yes," he pressed on, his voice barely above a whisper. "Do you understand? There can be no leaks."

His desperation mirrored my own. "I won't tell a soul, I swear," I breathed out, sealing our pact with a promise.

Leaning even closer, Samuel's voice dropped to a mere murmur. "We'll proceed with the wedding, play every part perfectly. But just before the ceremony, here's the twist." My eyes widened as he unfolded the audacious scheme, its daring nature sending a thrilling shiver down my spine. "It will appear that our enemies orchestrated the disruption, allowing us both to escape this fate without suspicion."

"And the men involved in the escape—are they reliable?" I asked, my voice trembling ever so slightly, not from fear but from the sheer audacity of our plan.

"They're my brother and his crew," Samuel reassured me, his confidence unshakable. "They'll protect you. No harm will come to you."

"Then I'm in," I declared without a second thought, my resolve steeling like a sword. "I'll do anything to avoid marrying you."

A laugh escaped Samuel's lips, momentarily easing the severity of the moment. "You're not easy on my ego," he said, a hint of relief lacing his laughter. In that instant, it became clear that he, too, longed to be free, to make a life most likely with the woman at his penthouse.

Agreeing to his dangerous plan, we shared a conspiratorial smile, our burden lightened by the shared secret. The stakes were high, but so were our hopes of getting out of this marriage. In that quiet corner of his restaurant, under the soft lighting and amidst the weight of our family's expectations, we forged a bond that would defy tradition and set us both free, and I couldn't wait until it happened.

5

I strode into the room, slung my phone into the faraday cage, and plopped down next to Valley. He'd gotten the same unexpected call to this meeting. Leather shot me his usual icy glare, but at least Player wasn't joining in today. Part of me hoped Leather would just throw a punch and get it over with; a good brawl might clear the air.

"You figure this is about a run?" Valley asked, tipping his chair back, eyes narrowed in curiosity. Invites like this usually meant something big; we weren't senior members, so something was up.

"Couldn't be anything else," I said, as Patch shuffled in, looking like he'd wrestled a bear. The mess with Katherine and Caden had really done a number on him.

"Let's dive in," Patch announced, resting his arms on the table and fixing his gaze on Scotch. "Any heat from our tangle with the Fire Dragons?"

"Clean," Scotch reported, a smirk playing on his lips. "Cops chalked it up to rival club drama. No leads, no interest and cased closed on their end."

"So, Papa Bears out for the count? No more trouble from the Fire Dragons?" Player chimed in, leaning forward.

Patch exhaled sharply. "Wish that were true, but Sarah's saying Papa Bear's grandson, Drago, is stirring up his own trouble with the Dragon Fire MC down in Georgia. Kid was on the outs with his grandaddy, started his own club and looking to expand. He'd made up with Papa Bear not long before everything went down."

"That's our blowback, then. He's eyeing South Carolina and Florida," Harker cut in. "He'll be out for revenge. Try to take our territory."

"Already warned Devil and Panther. But that's not why we're here." Patch flicked open a folder. "We got a high-stakes job. It's risky."

Leather perked up, leaning forward, his interest piqued. "Oh, yeah, risky how?"

Patch's gaze swept the room. "Samuel's paying big to disrupt his wedding this weekend. He's marrying off to honor a contract with Vittorio Amato's granddaughter—a mafia tie he wants to cut without starting a war."

"What's the play?" Player asked, suddenly all ears.

"I'll be on the inside as a guest. I'll help the bride—*who is on board with the plan*—escape through some tunnels during a distraction. You guys will handle the fireworks outside to make that happen. Player, you're on extraction at the designated location." Patch laid out the plan, his voice steady, unworried. But this was more than just risky, it was outright dangerous.

Jonesy shook his head, saying what I was thinking. "Messing with the Mafia, man. That's no joke."

"We go in clean. No colors, no faces, ditch the wheels after," Patch insisted, his gaze once again sweeping the room. "He's throwing two million our way, plus another mill to keep the woman hidden while he sorts things out. All heat goes to another mafia family."

Hillbilly whistled. "Hell of a payday."

Patch smirked. "She's under our roof till it cools down." His gaze flicked to me and Valley. "You two got babysitting duty. Just pretend she's your new flavor of the week or something. You two can figure it out."

I stifled a groan. Babysitting a likely spoiled mafia princess was the last thing I needed. "Understood," I grunted, not daring to argue.

"Word of this doesn't leave this room," Patch's voice hardened. "Not even to our own brothers."

Vain, looking better since getting back with Lana, raised an eyebrow. "Seriously?"

"Vittorio will make it worth someone's while to find her. Can't risk it," Patch stated flatly, then stood. "I'll set another meeting for Friday. Gotta get moving; Katherine and I are off to see Caden."

"He doing good? Getting bigger?" Jonesy asked, a slight smile breaking his usual stern expression.

"Better every day. Should be home soon," Patch replied, a rare warmth in his tone.

As everyone filtered out of the room, I looked at Valley, who grumbled, "She's probably going to be a bitch. That's why we got stuck with her, and now we gotta pretend to be into her."

"Agreed. Why else would Samuel want to ditch her, but when given an order..."

"Yeah, I know," Valley agreed, "But that doesn't mean I have to like it."

I nodded as we made our way back out into the common room. This is something I just didn't need right now. My mind was too far gone with visions of a redheaded ghost.

Valley nudged me, pulling me back to reality. "C'mon, let's grab a beer. We might as well enjoy the calm before the storm."

As we walked over to the bar, I couldn't shake the feeling that this job was going to change everything.

6

Hadleigh

Today was the day I was supposed to marry Samuel—or so everyone believed. I smiled, alone in my secret, a secret too dangerous to share. As I stood in the bridal room, surrounded by relatives, my heart wasn't pounding with the excitement of my nuptials but with anticipation of what was to come.

"Oh, Hadleigh, you look so beautiful," Lizzie gushed, scanning me from head to toe. "And Samuel! He's even more handsome than I remember. You're so lucky, Hadleigh. He won't be able to take his eyes off you."

I managed a tight smile, knowing well where Samuel's gaze truly lay—not on me. But that was a truth I harbored closely and would never reveal. My escape from this farce of a wedding was moments away.

The room buzzed with the chatter of my female relatives, their eyes gleaming with pride. But their smiles were soon to disappear.

It was time.

"Mother," I managed to say, keeping my voice steady. "I need some fresh air because I feel faint from all the excitement. Can I slip out to the garden for a moment alone, just to collect myself?" The private garden was part of Samuel's sprawling estate, secluded and perfect for what was planned next.

"Take Lizzie with you, dear," my mother suggested, "in case you need help with your dress."

I couldn't have that, but I couldn't argue it would look suspicious. "Okay," I agreed, masking my desperation. I needed to ditch Lizzie—fast.

As we stepped into the coolness of the garden, I reassured myself that everything would go as planned. I wouldn't need help with the dress because its train remained unattached, allowing me more freedom to move—*and to flee.*

Making idle conversation, I steered Lizzie towards the garden's ornate swing. "Lizzie, could you grab me some Tylenol from inside? I'm starting to get a headache," I said, feigning a wince.

"Of course, be right back!" she replied, her smile unwavering. She hurried off, thankfully more gullible than I had hoped.

No sooner had Lizzie disappeared than the sharp crack of gunshots pierced the air. My heart leaped into my throat as the bushes before me parted. A man with an eye patch, wearing a suit, appeared, signaling urgently. "This way, now!" he hissed.

My legs, fueled by a mix of fear and adrenaline, carried me after him through a labyrinth of tunnels. He finally halted, shoving the door open to reveal sunlight. "Run straight through those trees toward the road. A van will pick you up and whatever you do, don't slow down," he barked, giving me a slight push.

I burst into the clearing, my veil flapping wildly behind me. The promised van barreled towards me, slowing just enough for a hand to reach out and pull me inside. I collapsed onto the floor, laughter bubbling up from my relief that everything went as planned.

As the van sped away, a familiar voice cut through my

exhilaration. "Haddie?"

West Virginia Midnight
The Devil's House

Player, Teach and I sat in the van waiting on Patch's command to move, each of us buzzing with the kind of tension that comes when you're flirting with disaster. The mafia wasn't known for forgiveness; if they caught us, it'd be a bullet, no questions asked.

"It's time," Player announced from the driver's seat, revving the engine and slowly pulling out of our hiding spot towards the designated meeting point.

As we approached, I could see a panicked figure running towards us, her elaborate wedding dress flowing around her legs. "Now!" Player yelled, and I threw open the van door and reached out to grab the woman's hand, yanking her into the vehicle.

She stumbled and fell in a heap of lace as we sped away, her laughter ringing sharp and wild. A chill shot through me. That laugh... it was all too familiar. As she tore off her bridal veil, revealing fiery red hair, her face peppered with freckles, my heart stalled. "Haddie?" I whispered in disbelief.

Her eyes, wide with shock, met mine. "Kaven?"

A surge of happiness washed over me, quickly poisoned by the bitter sting of reality—she was supposed to be someone else's bride. Jealousy clenched my jaw tight. "You two know each other?" Player's voice cut through, eyes flicking to mine in the rearview mirror.

"I thought I did." My words felt heavy, watching the hurt cloud her face as she retreated, her gaze wounded and questioning.

I fought the urge to pull her close, to feel her against me like before.

But it was clear, whatever I felt back at that waterfall wasn't mutual. The van thrummed with the murmur of conversation from Player and Teach up front; the road stretching before us as we sped to the next phase of our plan. Haddie and I sat in silence, our eyes locked on one another until the van slowed down.

"We're swapping rides. Get ready," I announced as we rolled to a stop.

Haddie nodded, her face a mask as she followed me to the new vehicle. Patch was already there, scanning her with a keen eye. "Any trouble?" he asked.

"Smooth as whiskey neat," Player threw with a grin. "Girls got a set of legs on her," he chuckled, throwing her a wink.

Haddie offered a small, fleeting smile, which faded as she caught my stern look. Patch barked, "Let's move," and climbed into the driver's seat.

As Valley made to sit next to Haddie, I stepped in, claiming the spot with a silent claim of possession. My heart was a traitor, still bound to her despite the anger.

"You don't have to shove," Valley grumbled, settling behind us.

"I'm Valley and you are?" He reached over, tapping her shoulder.

"Hadleigh," she returned, her smile lighting up the dim interior.

Valley nodded, his tone friendly but cautious. "Looks like Midnight and I are watching over you while you're here."

Haddie's eyes flicked to mine, hardening slightly. "I'll try not to be any trouble."

"Just don't run," I said low, for her ears only. "Seems you've got a knack for it."

"Like you have a knack for acting like a jerk," she shot back, her voice soft but fierce.

Silence fell, thick and unresolved, as the van hurtled down the highway back to the clubhouse. And as I looked at her from the corner of my eye, looking at her in that wedding dress, that huge diamond gracing her finger, the hurt built up even more. She knew all along that we couldn't move forward, but didn't tell me, and let me fall for her.

That fucking pisses me off and makes me so damn angry at her.

Dread hung heavy in the van, my head spinning with a clutter of thoughts. I could feel her presence beside me, her tension matching mine. Player turned up the radio to drown out the silence, but it just bounced back, more stifling than ever. Each passing minute seemed to drag out into an hour, making the ride feel longer and more excruciating.

We arrived at the clubhouse as the sun was going down; the building was standing tall amidst the wooded landscape. "Home sweet home," Patch grumbled, swinging open the van's door. The rest of us shuffled out, relief that the job went off without a hitch, well for them maybe, but for me not so much.

7

Hadleigh

The moment my eyes met Kaven's, I thought fate had finally remembered us. Joy surged through me, so pure and so fierce. But it shattered just as quickly, crumbling under the weight of his gaze, turning from warmth to ice. God, how I ached to cross the space between us, to feel his arms shut out the world. Yet, his coldness wrapped tighter than any embrace, silencing me, freezing the tears before they could betray my pain.

Throughout the ride to their clubhouse, our eyes warred, mine pleading, his steeled with a hurt that seemed to calcify with every glance. The wedding dress must have screamed betrayal to him. Yes, I hadn't said goodbye, had left him to marry another man, and was never upfront with him about my life. His anger is justified, but couldn't he see the chains I was breaking just to breathe?

I rested a hand on my stomach, the secret within me heavy. Should I tell him? No, I couldn't—not yet. I wouldn't bind him to me with guilt or duty. My child and I were nobody's obligation. I loved Kaven, truly, but not enough to accept scorn as affection.

By the time the van veered onto a narrow side road, the setting sun mirrored my own exhaustion, both mental and physical. When we stopped in front of a looming warehouse, Kaven's touch sparked electricity as he guided me out. "Follow me," he commanded, releasing me as abruptly as he'd held me, and strode toward a side entrance.

His steps seemed to scream with a silent challenge as they pounded the ground; mine was defiance. I followed him through the door he held open, his face a mask of stone. My patience snapped. "If I'm such a burden, maybe you should let your friend take over," I spat, not willing to deal with this right now. Maybe come morning we could talk once things sink in.

"Drop the attitude, Haddie, and do what you're told," he shot back, resuming his march down the hallway.

"I'm not your prisoner, Kaven," I retorted. "I'm here under this club's protection, not to endure your bitterness." Pushing past him, I stormed into the room he'd led me to—a bedroom that would be my home for the next few months.

He grabbed my arm, a harsh retort on his lips, but a voice from the doorway cut him off. "Am I interrupting?" A woman, impossibly beautiful with a warm smile and a dog by her side, stepped in. "Patch sent me to help Hadleigh get settled and order what she needs." She waved a laptop in her hand. "I'm Ava."

Kaven's grip loosened, and he stepped back. "We'll talk more after," he muttered, his exit swift, leaving tension thick behind him.

Ava watched Kaven leave with a curious look on her face before moving into the room, her presence like a breath of fresh air after the last several hours. "Let's see what we can do to make you comfortable, Hadleigh."

As Ava set up her laptop on the small desk, I exhaled the storm Kaven had stirred. Why did things just keep getting more complicated?

Ava noticed my sigh and glanced at me, her eyes softening. "Is everything okay?" she asked, the tone in her voice indicating that she already knew the answer.

"I..." I paused, looking for the right words to encapsulate the whirlwind of emotions storming inside me. "I've been better," I admitted, sinking down onto the edge of the bed.

Ava nodded sympathetically. "I understand, situations like this can be... difficult," she acknowledged. "But Midnight and Valley are both great guys and you're in good hands."

"I don't know about that," I mumbled to myself almost before she finished her sentence.

Ava's eyebrows furrowed at my words, but she said nothing more on the subject as she pulled another chair up to the desk. "Have a seat and shop away," she said with a smile, her eyes saying she understood something else was at play here but wouldn't pry.

Ava was my lifeline. Her warm-hearted banter offered an escape from my thoughts, a beacon amidst swirling uncertainties. She helped me order clothes and essentials while sharing stories that often had me laughing. She was a sweet woman—kind, comforting—as if she, too, had known pain and used it to make herself stronger.

Yet despite her soothing presence, Ava couldn't erase Kaven's shadow that hung heavily over me or the bitter taste of our last confrontation. His silent accusation had burrowed deep into my skin, prickling like tiny needles every time I remembered it and it stung.

I slammed out the door, my back hitting the brick wall with a thud as I tried to reel in my temper. Mama would've knocked me across the

Midnight

room for laying hands on a woman, no matter the provocation. But goddamn, this mess with Haddie was fraying my edges bad, making me do shit I wouldn't normally do.

I still wanted her, damn me for it. It was driving me nuts.

Valley came up, leaning against the wall beside me, oblivious to the storm inside me. "Hey, man. Patch laid down the rule—one of us has gotta bunk next to her room every night. Make it look personal since the rooms adjoin."

Without a beat, I shot back, "I'll take it. Easier than shuffling around."

Valley raised his eyebrows, nonchalant as ever. "Cool with me. She's not what I expected, though. Thought she'd be some high-maintenance model type, but she's... nice. Kinda cute too, with that red hair, freckles, and did you notice that slight overbite when she smiled? You know what they say about redheads in the sheets," he chuckled, shaking his head, giving a low whistle.

I snapped, my voice a low growl. "Don't even think about it, Valley." My warning was clear—back the hell off.

He faced me, probing with those sharp eyes of his. "What's up with you and her? You know her, don't you?" When I didn't respond, realization dawned on him. "It's her, isn't it? The chick from South Carolina."

I nodded, barely. Trust Valley to piece it together. "Yeah, but it's over now. Keep it zipped."

Valley pushed, unable to let it be. "You're pissed she left you to marry Samuel, huh? Maybe she didn't have a choice, brother."

I clenched my fists, the anger again bubbling up. "There's always a choice, Valley. She could've been straight with me." He didn't get it, couldn't understand the depth of the connection Haddie and I had—or what I thought we had.

After a tense pause, Valley dropped the subject. "Alright, you handle nights, and we'll sort the day shift tomorrow."

"Yeah," I grunted, my energy spent. "It's been a long day."

"Don't I know it? I'm off to find Tracy, blow off some steam," Valley tossed over his shoulder as he headed inside.

I stayed out a bit longer, staring up at the creeping dusk, feeling the weight of the day press down. Finally, I headed back in to see if

Ava and Haddie had finished up. I'm sure she was hungry, so I'd take her to get something to eat. But as I moved, part of me dreaded seeing Haddie again, knowing all the unresolved shit that lay between us like landmines.

Hadleigh

"I think that's everything," **I said to Ava,** a sense of relief washing over me. I had meticulously ordered every item I might need during my stay here—from clothes to toiletries—ensuring that I had chosen garments that would accommodate my growing pregnancy over the next few months.

Ava, her eyes flickering with kindness, closed the laptop with a resounding thud. "It seems we're around the same size, so I can lend you some clothes to get by," she offered, her gaze unconsciously drawn to my wedding dress. I appreciated her tactful silence, refraining from prying into matters I knew were best left untouched.

There was an undeniable warmth in her presence, and I couldn't help but feel at ease around her. Emboldened by this newfound comfort, I ventured to ask, "I'll go stir-crazy without something to keep my hands busy. What do you suggest?" I ventured, hoping for a distraction.

"What do you like to do? Any hobbies?" she inquired.

"Plants, or something outdoors," I replied, my thoughts drifting to the feel of soil between my fingers.

"Plants?" she pondered for a moment, her brow furrowing in

concentration, before a spark of recollection ignited in her eyes. "Hmm, there's an old greenhouse near Ashby's barn. It's been neglected but, with a bit of love and care, it could be brought back to life. We could get whatever you need to start fixing it up," she proposed.

A smile stretched across my face, though I restrained myself from embracing her in gratitude. "Ava, that sounds perfect," I gushed, already envisioning the joy of resurrecting the dilapidated greenhouse and nurturing life within its walls.

Just then, her dog Hobo barked at her feet, breaking the moment. Ava chuckled and bent down to pat him, her laughter echoing softly in the room. "Better take him out now; that's his subtle hint," she joked, grabbing the laptop and heading towards the door. "I'll show you the greenhouse first thing tomorrow."

"Thank you for everything," I expressed sincerely as made her way toward the door.

"No problem, happy to do it. I'll see you in the morning," she promised before disappearing, just as Kaven reentered the room, his demeanor lifeless as a corpse.

"Let's grab something to eat," he suggested, his enthusiasm barely registering on his impassive face.

I approached the dresser, searching through the drawers until I found a dress that would suffice, albeit a tad loose. Holding it up to my frame, I declared, "Let me change out of this wedding gown first," I said, eager to shed the heavy layers.

"Yeah, good idea," he retorted sharply, his eyes dark with an emotion that at first was hard to read, but then I detected a flicker of pure jealousy beneath his stern façade—a sign he still cared.

Heading toward the bathroom, I suddenly realized that I would require assistance. Let's see how he handles this, I thought mischievously. Turning back to face him, a smile played on my lips as I requested, "I need you to unzip me and help me out of this dress. I'm practically sewn into this thing."

"What?" he whispered, his voice barely audible.

"I'm trapped in this gown like a silk package. I truly need your help," I insisted, stealing a glance over my shoulder to find him frozen by the doorway. "Come on, Kaven, you're well acquainted with every inch of my body. It's not a big deal."

Anticipation coursed through me as I heard his tentative footsteps approaching. Standing behind me, his hands gingerly settled on my waist, causing my breath to hitch at the proximity of his lips to my skin. Slowly, his fingers grazed the nape of my neck, slipping beneath the neckline of the dress. Then, with an abrupt tearing sound and a muttered curse, he forcefully ripped the fragile fabric down my back.

In that moment, time seemed to halt as our bodies remained tethered together. The air crackled with electricity, and I struggled to catch my breath.

Swallowing a gasp, I whirled around to face him, my eyes wide as he cast away the torn shreds of fabric. His features were contorted in a blend of anger and desire, his chest heaving with each breath. Kaven's gaze locked onto mine; his eyes filled with an intensity that made my heart pound in my chest.

I stood there, half-naked and frozen under his penetrating gaze. "Kaven," I breathed out, suddenly aware of the goosebumps prickling on my skin. "Why—"

"Quiet," he interrupted harshly, his hand reaching out to caress the bare curve of my shoulder where the wedding dress once was. His touch was a burning brand against my flesh, igniting sparks of heat that consumed me wholly.

"I couldn't stand it anymore," he confessed in a bitter voice, pulling me closer until we were a hair's breadth apart. "Seeing you in that dress... knowing... that you..." His broken confession reverberated around the room, amplifying the tension. "That you had someone else all along."

His hands slid further down my arms, leaving a burning trail in their wake as my skin tingled where he touched. His gaze roved over my face, a storm of emotions dancing in his eyes.

"I need to go," he muttered suddenly, pulling away abruptly. The sudden loss of contact left me reeling as I reached out to grab the bed for support. His words hung between us like a thick veil, reminding me of how strong our connection was. "I'll wait by the door."

"Kaven," I called out softly, watching as he walked toward the door. His back was stiff with tension, his every move radiating unease. "Can't we talk about this?" I asked, although I suspected the answers could only complicate things further, since he was so angry.

He paused by the entrance but didn't turn around to look at me.

His knuckles whitened as he gripped the handle, before he flung the door open and slamming it closed behind him, leaving me alone.

8

The Devil's House
West Virginia
Midnight

I grumbled, shifting on the uncomfortable bed. The sheets slipped from my naked body, pooling on the floor when I shifted after hearing a noise by the door. Poised in the doorway was Haddie, her hand tracing a path down her equally naked body as her eyes ran over me, a wicked smile on her face. "Haddie," My voice was husky, thick with lust as I watched her tease herself with an insinuating finger before raising it to her lips.

She sauntered towards me, and I found myself holding my breath, struck by the sheer force of how fucking beautiful she was, and her eyes held mine captive, her gaze never wavering. As she reached the bed, she bent down to press her lips against mine, her hands firmly guiding me onto my back as she claimed her position above me. Her lips moved lower, leaving a trail of tingling sensation down my neck and chest.

She loved the power she held over me. I had seen this in women before, but Haddie was different; she held my heart hostage with every glance she sent my way. Her actions were slow and deliberate, sending a wave of anticipation through me. "Haddie?" My voice was barely audible as I threaded my fingers through her hair—liquid fire, relishing the heat building inside my body.

Her soft tongue worked wonders on my skin as she took me into her mouth, her moans vibrating against me. "Haddie," I called out again through gritted teeth, but she didn't respond. Our eyes remained locked as she continued to work over me, stirring a storm of pleasure so intense that when it finally hit its peak, I found myself shaking uncontrollably.

"Damn!" I cried out, sitting upright in bed abruptly. My heart pounded in my chest as I took in the mess around me. "What the fuck?" My voice sounded foreign to my ears; it had all been a dream. I hadn't done this shit since I was a fucking teenager.

With a heavy sigh, I slipped out of bed to clean myself up. My gaze strayed towards the adjoining door that separated my dream from the tantalizing reality I knew existed. I was left with the whispers of what could have been, amplifying my longing for Haddie. This vivid dream had stirred the hunger I still held for her. I slipped on a pair of jeans and eyed the door separating us and, as if my feet had a mind of their own, headed that way.

I laid my hand on the doorknob, pressing my ear against the rough wood, straining for any sound. Silence. Haddie was out cold, so I eased the knob around, heart thumping a bit when the door swung open—unlocked. "Dammit, Haddie," I muttered under my breath. She's gotta know better than that. Anyone could've been in the connecting room and waltzed right in. I slipped inside, my feet whisper-quiet on the floor as I crept toward the bed. Just needed a glimpse of Haddie to settle my restless mind without waking her.

Just a peek and then I'd leave.

But the closer I got, the tighter my stomach knotted. The bed was empty. Flipping on the lamp, the harsh truth hit me—*she wasn't here*. "Shit." Had she bolted? I rushed to the window, heart racing, just in time to catch a small shadow darting into the woods.

Cursing under my breath, I hurried to slip on some shoes and hurried outside, tracking her path. No way was I gonna shout and tip anyone off; I was supposed to be watching Haddie. If she got lost or worse, it'd be on my head. And the last thing I needed was to rile up Patch—he was a ticking bomb lately.

There she was ahead, slipping through the dark like a cat, silent and sure. I couldn't help but shake my head; darkness was Haddie's ally, not her enemy. Guess that's one of the million reasons we meshed so well.

At last, she paused by a creek, settling by a tree to dip her toes into the cool stream. I hung back, hidden, watching her. She wasn't running away; she was searching for peace. So, I planted myself on the ground, keeping her in my sight for hours, sharing the quiet night without her knowing. It was calm, contemplative.

Together, yet apart.

When she finally stood to head back, I trailed her at a distance, making sure she was safely back at the clubhouse before I even thought about returning to my room. Alone again, the ache of her absence dug deep, and I spent the night parked by our shared door, too damn stubborn to bridge the gap between us. But I'd be watching, always near—*there was no help for it.*

9

My fist came down hard on the desk, reverberating through the room. Rage surged through me, fiercer than any storm. My granddaughter was out there, in the clutches of unknown enemies, and the mere thought of her in danger ignited a ferocious resolve within me. "If they so much as hurt a hair on her head, their deaths will be long and pleading," I seethed, my voice a low growl. "They'll beg for the end, but their torment will be far from over."

"Surely they left some clue behind," I bellowed, eyes sweeping over the anxious faces of the men crowded in my office.

Tony shifted uncomfortably under my glare. "We've combed the entire estate with Samuel's team. The last footage shows her strolling into the garden with Lizzie, then she just disappears," he reported, his voice tense.

Frustration clawed at me. I had stationed guards at every possible breach, especially at Hadleigh's door. Yet, here we were grappling with the reality of her disappearance, the whispered threats against our alliance now manifesting into my worst fears. "And the back gate?" I snapped.

"Several of Samuel's guards were found dead. The cameras were shot out—it's likely that's where they took her out," Tony continued, a grim note in his tone.

"How did they get inside the walls? There must have been accomplices inside," I roared, my disdain for incompetence clear. "Find Hadleigh. Bring me those responsible!" I waved dismissively, signaling them to execute their tasks. To me, Hadleigh was more than a granddaughter; she was the child I helped raise after her father's untimely death, irreplaceable and cherished deeply.

Just then, a knock on the door interrupted my thoughts. My guard peeked in. "Samuel is here," he announced with a nod. Despite the attack on his home and the loss of his men, Samuel's primary concern was assisting in our search—a grace not lost on me.

"Any news?" Samuel asked, settling into a chair across from me.

"It's as if she vanished into thin air," I admitted. The weight of my worry was clear in my tone.

"My suspicion is the Toro family. They've vowed revenge since we took most of their territory. This alliance would be their end," Samuel speculated calmly. "We're tracking down their lieutenants for questioning."

"Good strategy," I acknowledged with a brief smile, the first in hours. "While you do that, I'll have my men detain some from the Santiago clan. They're also on my radar."

"Don't worry, we'll find her," Samuel reassured, his confidence unshaken.

A heavy sigh escaped me. "The thought of what they might be doing to her, the terror she must be feeling... it's unbearable."

"They wouldn't dare to harm her, not when they know the vengeance we would unleash," Samuel asserted as he stood to leave. "They'll likely keep her hidden to disrupt any chance of an alliance by marriage."

I chuckled darkly, a humorless sound. "You're trying to ease my mind, and I appreciate it, Samuel. But we both know the harsh realities of our world."

"I'll keep you informed of any developments," he promised, then exited.

Leaning back in my chair, I let my head fall back, eyes closed in momentary surrender to exhaustion. One thing was crystal clear in my mind: giving up was not an option. I would bring Hadleigh home, no matter the cost.

10

Hadleigh

I might as well be sitting alone, I thought, pushing my eggs around the plate. Morning sickness and stress had ruined my appetite. Kaven sat silent, not even glancing my way, his eyes glued to his phone. It had been this way since the incident with the wedding dress yesterday. Just as I brought the toast to my lips, a syrupy voice cut through the morning din.

"Morning, sweetie."

A woman with too much perfume and apparently poor eyesight took a seat next to Kaven, draping her arm around his waist and nestling into his side like she belonged there.

"Morning, Bunny," Kaven responded, his smile all teeth and a warmth I hadn't seen since seeing him again. He didn't bother to move her arms away, letting her lean into him like I wasn't even there. My grip on the toast tightened until it crumbled in my hand. The clubhouse was alive with the morning hustle of club members, the smell of coffee and bacon, but all I could focus on was the growing knot of anger in my stomach.

He had some nerve treating me this way over things I couldn't control when he obviously hadn't been lonely during our separation.

My mother was spot on about men.

I shot a glance around the room, spotting Valley by the door. Standing up, I faced the cozy pair with a forced, sunny smile. "I'll leave you two to it then," I said, my voice sharp as shattered glass. "I see Valley, and it's obvious you could use some free time. Enjoy."

Kaven stood, but I was quicker. I walked over to Valley. "I need some air. Will you show me around?"

Valley's eyes darted to Kaven, then back to me, a hint of amusement in his gaze. "Sure," he agreed, though his voice suggested he knew he was stepping into a minefield.

"I can take you," Kaven insisted, reaching for my arm.

I jerked away, shaking him off with a fake smile. "No, enjoy your breakfast and your company. I wouldn't dream of interrupting your morning cuddles, sweetie." I glanced around him, seeing Bunny watching us curiously, and added, "Valley's got me on this, so no worries. Now hurry back and finish what you started."

Hooking my arm through Valley's, I pulled him toward the door, Kaven's gaze scorching our backs. Valley chuckled lowly. "You're gonna get me in trouble."

"He treats me like an inconvenience," I snapped as we stepped outside. "And I don't have to stand for it. Besides, you're stuck babysitting me too, right? Let's give him a bit of 'me' time. Maybe it'll fix his attitude."

Valley laughed, a deep rumbling sound. "You've got fire, Hadleigh, I like it."

I shrugged off the compliment. "I'm sick of my life being manipulated by those around me. It's exhausting."

Outside, the air was fresh, but did little to soothe my frayed nerves. We sat at the worn picnic table, the wood rough under my hands. "I think I'm just overwhelmed with everything," I confessed, my voice dropping.

Valley stretched out, relaxed in the early morning sun. "Understandable. This place isn't much, but it's home. Guess it's quite the change from what you're used to?"

I laughed bitterly. "Big and shiny doesn't mean it's not a cage. Money's worthless if it's choking you."

Valley tugged at a loose strand of my hair, smiling. "You're nothing like I expected."

A loud bang startled us, and Valley was instantly on his feet. Kaven leaned against the clubhouse wall, his expression thunderous. The door behind him had slammed shut from his entrance.

Ignoring him, I turned to Valley. "I think I need that walk now. Ava mentioned an old greenhouse?"

As if summoned, Ava appeared down the path, her dog trotting beside her and a towering man with a cat in his arms by her side. She waved as they approached. "Morning, Hadleigh! Ashby here was just hearing about your interest in the greenhouse."

Ashby, his hand petting the cat, eyed me skeptically. "It's a lot of work. You'll need extra hands."

Valley stepped up. "We've got it covered, Scotch. Me and Midnight are on it."

"Then have at it." Ashby shrugged dismissively and kissed Ava before turning away, heading back to the clubhouse.

Ava gestured towards a narrow path. "Let's go check it out."

Kaven's voice, suddenly close behind me, made me stiffen. "I'll shadow. Valley, you're needed inside."

Valley smirked at him, raising an eyebrow. "Sure thing. Later, Hadleigh... Ava," he said, heading inside.

With a glare that could cut steel, I turned away from Kaven and walked beside Ava, determined not to let him ruin another moment of my life.

West Virginia Midnight

Why did I let Bunny cling to me like that? Honestly, I had no clue. Maybe I was just being a petty ass, and I should've seen Haddie not taking my shit coming. She wasn't the type to just let that slide without clapping back.

And man, when I saw Valley touching her hair outside, it nearly drove me insane. I wanted to march over there and snap his fingers off. But I had to play it cool. If I caused a scene or pushed Haddie too far, Patch would boot me from my duty. She made it clear she wasn't a prisoner, and with Samuel shelling out big bucks for her safety, Patch wasn't about to let my petty grudges mess that up.

Despite the rollercoaster we were on, staying away from Haddie wasn't an option for me. Her presence was like a drug—intoxicating and impossible to quit. And now, here I was, following her and Ava to a greenhouse? I didn't even know we had one here. Guess that's because I hardly ever came to this part of the grounds. It was Scotch's domain, and he liked his solitude.

"It's over here," Ava said, leading us through the undergrowth to where the old greenhouse stood, all swallowed by nature. The glass panes were clouded with age, and vines wrapped around the frame like nature's chains. "You can see it's a bit wild and going to need some serious TLC."

"It just needs a little love," Haddie chimed in, her face lighting up as she waded through the brush. That's one thing I learned in our short time together—she's got a thing for all things green and growing.

"Watch yourself, Haddie," I warned her. "You're not exactly dressed for bushwhacking. Don't wanna end up with a snake bite, do you?"

I braced for a snappish comeback, but instead, she turned to Ava. "He's right, I need to change. Got any clothes I can have that you won't mind getting destroyed? I'm eager to dive into this."

"Of course, I'll find you something," Ava offered. "I'll head back and gather some stuff while you explore."

"Thanks a ton, Ava," Haddie replied, stepping out of the thicket. "I'll just make a mental list of what I'll need and find you after."

Once Ava was gone, there we were—just me and Haddie. I watched her survey the ramshackle structure, her mind racing. The way she looked at that decrepit greenhouse, you'd think it was a palace. "You sure you want to tackle this?" I asked, peering over her shoulder.

She whirled on me, snapping, "Don't worry about it. I don't expect any help from you. Go find something—*or someone*—else to occupy your time. Let Valley handle it."

"Jealous, are we?" I retorted, a little sharper than I intended. "Last time I checked, you were almost married."

She spun around, her eyes blazing with a fire that could melt steel. "What's it to you?" she snapped. "You and Bunny have been... well, let's just say it's obvious. So don't act like you're the injured party, Kaven. You chose to be with someone else. My marriage was being forced on me, and I sure as hell didn't sleep with anyone else while we were apart."

She brushed past me, heading back to the path, her movements as fierce and determined as a storm.

"Haddie, you don't get it..." I started.

She stopped and glared back at me. "Just save it, Kaven. It's clear you don't know what you want or how you feel. And I can't fix that for you. Go see if Bunny can, because I've got enough on my plate!"

I stood there, dumbfounded, as she walked away. Damn it, Haddie was wrong. I knew exactly what I wanted and how I felt. And that was the real problem.

I watched her disappear into the trees, her silhouette becoming a ghost among the leaves. My heart pounded in my chest, a rhythm of regret and frustration. I had to figure out a way to break this cycle, to get past the anger at her.

But how?

She deceived me, or at least that's how I saw it, and if Samuel hadn't stopped the wedding, Haddie would have married him. I couldn't get past that no matter how hard I tried, but I couldn't move on either.

"Fuck and fuck again," I muttered under my breath as I kicked at the ground in frustration.

As I turned back to the greenhouse, a thought struck me. The place was a mess, much like my relationship with Haddie. Maybe, just maybe, if I could help her restore this forgotten place, it could be a start to fixing all this shit between us.

I ignored the voice inside my head that screamed, "You're gonna fuck this up!"

11

Hadleigh

I perched on a stool at the busy bar of the clubhouse, an intriguing yet foreign world unfolding around me. Ava, managing the bar with a deft hand, entertained my curiosity between orders, answering all my questions. The atmosphere bristled with the raw energy of a rougher crowd, one different from the world I came from. The room buzzed with loud music and louder conversations, the clack of pool balls breaking through their laughter.

I scanned the room, noting the dynamics on display between the females in the room. A few women wearing vests labeled as 'property' clung to men, asserting their places in this club. Others navigated the room, finding attention where it was welcomed. At a table, Kaven—here known as Midnight—was deeply engrossed in a card game, never once glancing my way.

Ava caught the direction of my gaze and chuckled. "Midnight, along with Patch and poor Ashby, are basically handing their wallets to Player tonight," she said, shaking her head. "I've no idea why they bother challenging him at poker."

I frowned, curious. "Why do they keep playing if he always wins?"

"Hope springs eternal," Ava chuckled, her eyes tracking a new couple entering. The man's gaze locked with Kaven's, his expression tightening with undisguised hostility. "Let's hope Leather keeps his anger in check tonight. He can be a hothead and impulsive."

"Trouble with Kaven?" I asked, sensing the tension between the two.

"You could say that," Ava murmured, pouring a drink with practiced ease. "Leather can't forgive him for the whole Aislynn saga, the whole thing was a mess."

My heart sank hearing her explanation. "Kaven was involved with her?"

Ava paused, considering her words. "Not necessarily involved. Midnight wanted her, and Aislynn chose Leather. After the fight and everything that went down, he left for South Carolina to take a breather and let things blow over."

Aislynn moved through the crowd, and I felt a sharp pang of envy. Kaven loved her, wanted her enough to fight over her. The sting of realization hit me, because he sure as hell wasn't fighting for me.

I was a rebound.

My chest tightened as I took in her perfect blonde features, almost doll like, what man wouldn't fall in love with her. My features were loud and brash next to her, and at this moment, I felt like a raggedy Ann doll. Not only had he been intimate with Bunny, but he was in love with someone.

A woman that wasn't me.

Taking a deep breath, I pushed the feeling away, trying to keep from suffocating on that new information.

I reminded myself who I was—Hadleigh Amato—and I wasn't insecure and jealous of other women; I wasn't brought up to feel sorry for myself. So, Kaven wasn't the man I thought he was, and the relationship I dreamed of was just that, *a dream*. My mistake in judgement and the consequence is mine to bear and I'm strong enough to go through it on my own.

Ava noticed my distant look. "Everything okay? You look a little pale."

I forced the brightest smile I could manage. "Absolutely. Just taking it all in. It's interesting learning about how the place runs."

At that moment, Aislynn approached us, her smile warm but cautious. "Braden mentioned you were here," she said, sliding onto the stool beside me. "I'm Aislynn."

Great, she was soft-spoken and sweet as well, a one-eighty from me.

Yep, I was the *"Trying to forget the one sex."*

Trying to keep the conversation light, I asked her about her life outside the clubhouse and her obvious pregnancy. As we spoke, her gaze darted occasionally to Leather, especially when a blonde woman flirted with him. The woman quickly retreated after a few sharp words from him, prompting Aislynn to mutter under her breath.

"What's that?" I asked, though I had a guess.

Aislynn sighed. "These women—the sweet butts—they know he's taken, and yet they push. It's exhausting."

"It's a challenge for them," I suggested. "But if he's committed and loves you, that's what matters."

"That's right," a pregnant brunette chimed in, joining us with a knowing smile. "Those bitches try to destroy relationships. Look at what they did to me and Scott, and almost succeeded. Don't buy into it, Aislynn."

"Easier said than done," she replied, still side-eyeing the blonde.

"I'm Lana," she introduced herself, with a playful glint in her eye. Her property vest dubbed her belonging to Vain. "So, which one is your man? I heard it could be Valley or Midnight, or is it both like a why choose kind of thing? You can tell us, we won't judge."

My cheeks warmed at the image her words conjured in my head. "Lana!" Ava laughed, shaking her head. "Why did you ask that?"

Lana just shrugged. "Hey, what single woman wouldn't want to be the meat between those two slices of bread? Our girl here is lucky, if that's the case, of course. *Is it?*"

What was I missing here? Before I could respond, Kaven was

suddenly by my side. "She's with me, no sandwich here," he announced, taking my hand. "Let's get some fresh air." I took his hand, only because I was curious about what was going on, and I ignored the part of my brain that asked the question: was he trying to make Aislynn jealous by saying he was with me?

Damn! This hurts.

I struggled to feign interest in poker, especially with Haddie in the room. My wallet couldn't keep up with Player, and with Leather's watchful gaze fixated on me like I was going to abduct Aislynn any second, I knew my time at the table was over, not that I had any more money to lose.

Despite our silence since our recent falling out, Haddie had my full attention, and I couldn't focus as long as she was near. Plus, it hadn't escaped my notice that several men in the room were eyeing her up like new candy. Haddie just had that extra something that caught your attention.

"Come on, Midnight, fold already," Player grumbled, his eyes fixed on me over his cards. "You're dragging this out longer than a Sunday sermon."

I glanced at my pitiful hand and tossed the cards onto the table. "I'm out," I muttered, leaning back in my chair.

Patch, let out a chuckle. "You've been out since you sat down, Midnight. Poker's not where your heads at."

Scotch took a swig from his glass and smirked. "Yeah, maybe you should stick closer to Hadleigh over there. Looks like she's got everyone's attention, including yours."

"Shut it, Scotch," I snapped, though my eyes involuntarily flicked to Haddie again. She was laughing at something Lana said, and the sight of her smile was enough to twist my insides.

"Leave him alone," Patch said, his tone more serious. "Everyone's got their distractions. Midnight's just happens to be wearing a dress tonight."

Player raked in the pot with a satisfied grin. "Distracted or not, I'm taking all your money tonight, brothers. So, who's in for another round?"

I pushed back from the table, standing up. "Not me. I've got other things on my mind."

As I walked away, I could hear the others ribbing each other, their laughter and taunts following me away from the table. I made my way over to Haddie, prepared to take a stool and do what Scotch suggested.

Approaching the women, I overheard a conversation between the ol' ladies that pissed me off. The suggestion that me, Haddie and Valley were all involved together incensed me. No matter our current status, I considered Haddie mine and mine only. I recognized her lost look at their questions, and it was my fault she was confused; I had neglected to inform her of our cover story. There was no way she would pretend to be with Valley, not happening.

Leading her outside, I hesitated before admitting, "Part of your cover here is that you're my girlfriend."

"Why you?" she questioned, her expression distant. "You don't want to be with me, and Valley doesn't mind, so why can't it be him?"

"Because, Haddie, we already know each other. It makes it easier," I replied, attempting to keep my temper in check.

She sighed, turning away, murmuring, "No, I thought we knew each other, but we don't."

"I wasn't the one who left, Haddie, remember?" I reminded her, puzzled by her calm demeanor. Something was off.

Suddenly, Bunny and Tammy interrupted, giggling suggestively. Where the hell did they come from? "How about we have some fun, baby? Only with two," Bunny purred, reaching for me, not seeing Haddie in the shadows.

"Bunny..." I started, but Haddie interrupted.

"No, you go ahead," she murmured, keeping her voice low for my ears only, her eyes distant. "This is only pretend and shouldn't stop you from enjoying yourself."

She turned to walk away, and I stopped her by taking her arm. "Haddie?"

She moved my hand off her arm and said over her shoulder as she continued walking, "I'm going to bed, so I'll be in for the night. Really, it's okay."

"Midnight, how about it?" Bunny pressed, reminding me of her presence behind me.

"Bunny, I'm not interested anymore. Things are different for me now," I replied, feeling the need to set boundaries. "I'm with Haddie."

"For real?" Bunny asked in disbelief. "That red-haired...." Her words trailed away because she knew better than to insult her.

"Yeah, now move on," I snapped, not liking Bunny insinuating Haddie was anything but beautiful.

It technically wasn't their fault; they didn't know any better since I hadn't set them straight. I never used to be one to turn down a good time, but things were different now. The sweet butts nodded in disappointment and retreated inside, mumbling about all the men getting taken.

My eyes went to where Haddie had faded into the darkness. Was she giving up on us? Could I blame her? I'd been pushing her away, unable to let go of my hurt. I'd let her believe I'd been with the sweet butts since her, so why did the thought of her moving on and letting go feel like losing a limb?

Valley emerged from the shadows, his voice cutting through the night. "You're messing this up, brother."

"Don't start, Valley," I warned, a desperate itch to find Haddie clawing at me like a drug addict deprived of a fix.

"Are you still hung up on Aislynn, using Hadleigh as a distraction?"

"Why would you even think that?" I shot back in disbelief that he thought something so stupid.

"Because if you cared about Hadleigh, you'd try to understand her perspective. Talk to her about what happened with Samuel," he reasoned. "Her family is the mafia, man. She couldn't just walk away, and Samuel didn't have to force her to run."

"She could have told me, given me a heads up before I let her get close," I countered stubbornly. "Or better yet, tell me so I could help her."

"If you can't forgive, let me step in. Why drag this out? It's not fair to her."

I eyed him suspiciously. "Why are you suddenly so eager to babysit? You got a thing for her?"

"No, and even if I did, I wouldn't touch that mess you two have," he assured me. "But this is going to blow up, and I don't want Patch coming after me when it does. I'm also on her security detail, remember?"

"It'll be fine. I've got it under control. Now, I need to make sure she got inside okay," I said, leaving Valley muttering about Patch burying us on the property as I walked away.

Heading towards her room, I jiggled the door handle and found it locked. "Haddie?" I called out, but there was no answer. "Haddie?" I tried again, louder this time. Her muted voice finally came from behind the door before it swung open.

"I'm going to bed, Kaven. I'm exhausted. Is it important?"

"What's wrong? If it's about the sweet butts—"

She cut me off with a sharp wave of her hand, her eyes narrowing with a determined glare. "No, Kaven, this isn't about them. Like I said, go have fun. It's not a big deal. I guess it's normal for a supposedly taken man to be with those women and it won't blow this ridiculous cover," she snapped.

"I wasn't going to go with them," I shot back, my voice rising.

"It's not my business either way," she replied with a forced, tight-lipped smile. "We had a brief affair and it's over. In a few months, I'll go back to my life, and all this will be forgotten."

"What the hell is wrong with you?" I snarled, my anger boiling over. "Do you really want me to go be with those women?"

She shrugged, her gaze piercing mine. "Won't bother me in the slightest."

"Fine, maybe I'll rethink my plans tonight," I growled, but I didn't budge from her door. Something had shifted in Haddie, and it was glaringly obvious—she was pulling back, no longer fighting. Normally she would've thrown a fit over the sweet butts hitting on me, but not tonight.

Tonight, she basically told me to fuck whoever I wanted with her blessing.

She shut the door with a solid click, and I let out a frustrated sigh. Pushing away from her door, I retreated to my room and listened at the connecting door, hearing nothing. I dropped onto the bed, staring up at the ceiling, my mind racing with frustration and confusion.

12

Hadleigh

I was doing my best to stay distant from Kaven, both physically and emotionally, but he wasn't making it easy. He insisted on helping me clear the area around the greenhouse, working silently side by side. Every time he tried to bring up something other than the greenhouse, I would immediately change the subject or walk away. The pain was raw, and I needed time—something he apparently wasn't willing to give me as he continued to shadow me ninety percent of the time. Asking for Valley instead did no good; Kaven just ignored my request, and I didn't want to have to see Patch. Honestly, the man scared me.

"Hadleigh?" A female voice pulled me from my thoughts as I sat on a stool at the bar, staring into space.

I turned to see a woman I hadn't met yet. "Yes," I replied.

"I'm Daphne," she introduced herself with a big smile. "I've missed meeting you the last few times I was here." She studied me for a second before saying, "You look so sad, and that just won't do. Not on my watch!"

"No, I'm fine, really," I assured her.

She glanced over at Kaven, who was talking with Valley, a shadow of worry crossing her face. "Midnight being a crappy boyfriend?" she asked, then continued before I could answer. "He needs a reminder that you have options. Come on," she ordered, taking my hand and pulling me into the crowd, leading me to a small area where people were dancing.

"It's okay," I shouted over the music, which seemed much louder in this corner of the room.

"It's not okay," she said, stopping in the middle of several men. "Now dance!"

Oh, what the hell. I hadn't danced in this kind of environment in a really long time, and this time I didn't have one of my grandfather's men watching my every move. There was a reason I was still a virgin when I met Kaven. And it wasn't like Kaven and I were really a couple, so what could it hurt?

I started swaying to the music, letting the beat and the energy of the room seep into my bones. The lights were dim, the air thick with the scent of perfume and alcohol. I didn't even realize when Daphne was replaced at my side by a blonde man who smiled at me, his eyes raking over my body. He was middle-aged and not a club member because he wasn't wearing a vest. He leaned down and said, "You're a cute one, strawberry shortcake."

I laughed because I had never been referred to as strawberry shortcake. Every other redheaded character out there, yes, but never her. Apparently, he took my humor as acceptance of his company because the next thing I knew, his hands had pulled me close to his body. That was a big fat no-no, and I put my hands up to push him away but only met air as his body was jerked away from mine.

I gasped, looking to find Kaven dragging him out the side door, Valley and some other men right behind him. "Oops, that wasn't supposed to happen," Daphne said, at my side once more. "Sometimes I forget how dangerous these men can get when they're jealous."

"I better go help him," I said, feeling a surge of guilt and responsibility.

Daphne grabbed my arm and led me back to the bar. "No, don't go out there. It won't do any good. The man still put his hands on you, and he should have known better. In this clubhouse, you check first, touch after," she explained. "It was obvious you weren't a hang around or sweet butt."

"Man, Midnight was fuming," Ava said from where she was leaning on the bar. "I've never seen his face look like that before."

"Looks like Midnight has it bad for Hadleigh," Daphne chuckled. "Now maybe he won't leave you alone at the bar."

"What happened?" Aislynn asked, coming up to us. "Braden sent me inside and said to wait for him, and he took off out back."

"Midnight's taking care of some handsy fellow," Daphne said, hugging her. "Guy touched his girl."

Seeing Aislynn put me back into a funk even though she wasn't to blame. Just looking at her made the hurt deeper, and I needed to be alone. "I better go and get a first aid kit from the kitchen," I lied, needing to escape.

"Good idea. Be ready to patch up your man. They like to be babied like that," Daphne said, her laugh ringing in my ears as I left the now much quieter room.

The kitchen was a welcome sanctuary from the loud common room. I leaned against the counter, taking deep breaths to steady my racing heart. The noise from the bar area was muffled here, giving me a moment to collect myself. My mind was a whirlpool of conflicting emotions—anger, confusion, longing. Kaven's presence was both a comfort and a torment.

Why did he have to be so damn protective? And why did that protectiveness make my heart ache with frustration because it was so damn confusing?

Footsteps echoed in the hallway, and I tensed, expecting Kaven to storm in. Instead, it was Valley, his expression a mix of concern and curiosity.

"Hey," he said softly, closing the door behind him. "You okay?"

"I'm fine," I lied, plastering on a weak smile. "Just needed a breather."

Valley studied me for a moment before nodding. "Midnight had to show the man his mistake, you know. That guy crossed a line, knowing he had no right to touch you."

"I know, Daphne explained," I sighed, feeling the weight of my situation pressing down on me. "But it's more complicated than that, Valley. Like I said the other day, I'm overwhelmed with everything."

Valley leaned against the counter next to me, his gaze thoughtful. "He cares about you, Hadleigh, and he's not doing a great job of handling it."

"Yeah, well, caring isn't enough," I said bitterly, forcing myself not to cry and be pathetic.

We stood in silence for a few moments, the tension in the air thick. Finally, Valley spoke again, his tone gentle but firm.

"Maybe you need to talk to him. Really talk. Not just about the greenhouse or the club, but about what's going on between you two."

I looked at him and sighed, "Maybe you're right. But not tonight. I just can't. He makes it too hard."

He nodded, understanding. "Take your time. But don't take too long. Some things are worth fighting for and there is no use being miserable if you don't need to be."

With that, he gave me a reassuring smile and left, leaving me alone with my thoughts once more. I took a deep breath, trying to steady myself. I knew he was right, but right now, I needed to be alone.

My anger burned like hellfire at the sight of that asshole touching Haddie. I was already on edge when I saw her and Daphne start dancing. Haddie moved to the rhythm, lost in the music, and I couldn't take my eyes off her. I knew I wasn't alone in my admiration, which only fueled my rage.

I shot up from my seat.

"Take it easy, brother," Valley warned, his voice tense. "They're just dancing... oh shit."

"He's a dead man," I growled, storming over and yanking the guy away from her. I dragged him out the door.

"What the hell?" the man shouted, struggling to break free.

"You touched my property," I snarled, shoving him outside. He stumbled, scrambling to stand.

"No way, she wasn't wearing a property cut," he argued, confusion crossing his face.

"Should've asked first. You must be new here," I growled, my fist connecting with his face and knocking him back down.

He staggered to his feet and threw a punch. I easily dodged and hit him again, watching him hit the dirt, out cold. These hang arounds thought they had what it took to be one of us, but couldn't even handle a few punches.

"Well, that was boring," Hillbilly chuckled. "Guy couldn't fight his way out of a plastic wrap."

"Or he's pretending," Leather said, giving him a hard kick. "Nope, he's out cold. How's it feel having another man hit on your woman, even if you're only pretending?"

"For the last time, drop it, Leather. I've moved on, and so should you," I snapped, wishing he'd shut the hell up. We weren't pretending, dammit.

"Maybe you have, but until I'm sure you're on my radar," he replied, turning to leave.

"What are we doing with him?" Valley asked, pointing at the unconscious man.

"Fuck him," I spat, turning to go back inside and talk to Haddie. I had been trying to stay calm, waiting out the ice wall she'd built around herself, even though I wanted to break it wide open. The silent treatment was one thing, but enticing another man? That sent me into a rage.

Inside, I scanned the common room but didn't see her. She must have gone back to her room already. I took a moment to have a beer and calm down before trying to talk to her. We always seemed to end up fighting, and I hoped tonight would be different. I walked to her room and knocked on the door.

No answer.

Maybe she wasn't inside, so I turned the knob and discovered it was unlocked. I made a mental note to talk to her about locking her door. Without knocking, I walked in just as Haddie emerged from the bathroom, wearing only a towel. Her startled gasp at seeing me in her room caused the towel to slip to the floor, and my heart skipped a beat as my eyes took in every inch of her.

13

Hadleigh

I decided I needed a shower to help me relax. This situation with Kaven was driving me insane. The hot water cascading over my body provided some relief, but I was still hurt over everything that had unfolded over the last few days. Eventually, I turned off the water and wrapped a towel around me, leaving the bathroom to crawl into bed.

My breath caught in my throat as I yelped, seeing Kaven standing in the middle of the room. The towel slipped from my grasp and dropped to the floor. His eyes widened in surprise before boldly traveling down my body, lingering on my damp, glistening skin and the curves it revealed. Despite the hurt, I couldn't deny the thrill that his hungry gaze ignited inside me—a powerful blend of power and sexual attraction. So, I stood there, back straight and unashamed, staring right back at him.

"Why are you here?" I asked, trying to pretend he didn't affect me. "You need to leave."

Kaven took a step forward with purposeful strides, his eyes never leaving mine. As he closed the distance between us. He reached me, standing so close that I could feel the heat radiating from his body. "I don't think you really want me to leave," he whispered in my ear, before biting my ear lobe. "You enticed another man to get my attention and trust me, you have it."

"Kaven... I..."

Without breaking eye contact, he raised his hand and gently caressed my cheek before moving it down to my neck. His fingertips traced an electric path along my collarbone and then further down, teasingly circling one nipple before giving it an insistent pinch. A gasp escaped my lips, betraying how much this affected me.

Kaven smirked knowingly as his other hand found its way to my waist, pulling me closer until our bodies were pressed together. His erection strained against his jeans while our hips connected in an erotic dance of friction. My legs grew weak at the sensation of him getting harder because of me.

He suddenly spun me around so that my back was against his chest, and I could feel his length pressing into my lower back as he whispered hotly into my ear. "I want you, Haddie." The command in his voice sent shivers down my spine. I couldn't—*and wouldn't*—deny him, because that would deny me as well, and I had become addicted to the way he made me feel, dreamed of it every night since our last night together.

I would regret it later, not a doubt in my mind, but I'll just add it to the long list already in progress. Foolish and impulsive, Hadleigh strikes again.

No surprise here.

As Kaven's hands continued their sensual exploration, delicately skimming over my body as if I were the finest silk, I braced myself for the impending storm of passion that was about to overtake us both.

His fingers trailed lower, ghosting over my stomach, and I sucked in a sharp breath at the sensation. He pressed his lips to the sensitive spot behind my ear, his hot breath making me shiver. I leaned back against him, the feeling of his hard muscles providing a comforting yet exciting barrier.

He completely entranced me, enveloped by the heady scent of his cologne mixed with the underlying note of his own unique smell. His hands moved lower, sliding past my hips to grip the backs of my thighs, pulling me even tighter against him. He bent his head down, nuzzling my neck and placing the softest of kisses on my pulse point.

My knees felt weak, and I knew I wouldn't be able to stand much longer. Sensing this, he scooped me up effortlessly in his arms. He carried me to the bed, our eyes locking as he gently set me down on it. He hovered over me, removing his vest and tearing his t-shirt over his head, his dark eyes filled with desire and a promise of ecstasy that made my pulse race. Kaven leaned down to capture my lips in a searing kiss, his hands roaming over my body. Every inch of me came alive under his touch, intensifying the electrifying connection between us.

His tongue explored my mouth greedily, tasting, teasing and claiming me as his. His hand slipped between our bodies, finding my wetness with an instinctive precision that left me gasping against his mouth. I arched into him, craving more of his touch.

He broke the kiss, only to trail hot kisses along my jawline and neck, nipping and soothing in turn that left me writhing beneath him. His fingers dipped lower, sliding through the slick wetness he had elicited from me. With a moan, I opened my legs wider, silently pleading for him to fill the void within me.

Kaven answered my silent plea in his own time, withdrawing his fingers to unbuckle his pants. His arousal sprang free as he pushed the material down his legs, the sight of him causing an illicit thrill to run through me. The feeling of his hands reaching out to grip my thighs, holding me steady as he positioned himself at my entrance. His gaze met mine, dark and intense with unspoken promises.

Then he was pushing inside me in one smooth thrust, his size stretching me deliciously. A cry escaped my lips as I adjusted to his fullness, my back arching off the bed as pleasure coursed through me. His dark eyes bore into mine, taking in every reaction, every gasp, every moan.

"Look at me," he commanded, his voice low and husky with need. I did as I was told, locking my gaze on him. He started moving inside me then, each thrust bringing us closer to the edge. His pace was torturous—slow yet powerful, deliberate yet passionate.

His fingers dug into my hips, the slight sting only heightening the pleasure. Kaven's eyes never strayed from mine as he moved, his rhythm slow and relentless. The tenderness in his gaze was at odds with the possession in his movements, making me feel cherished and claimed all at once.

Flashes of heat coursed through me with each thrust, intensifying until it was all I could focus on. Kaven watched intently, seeming to take satisfaction in my reactions. Sweat beaded on his forehead, trickling down to mingle with the moisture on my skin.

Every stroke was calculated, designed to draw out the experience, increasing the need that pulsed between us. His hand moved around me, pressing into the small of my back, pulling me further onto him. With each thrust, he filled me completely, like the missing piece of a puzzle I didn't know was incomplete.

His eyes were darker now, black pools of desire that mirrored my need for him. Kaven's face was flushed with arousal, the usual coolness replaced by a burning intensity that only heightened my own response. I reached up to run my hands through his hair, holding him to me.

"Kaven..." I moaned his name like a prayer as he continued to move inside me. He responded by pressing his lips to mine in a fierce kiss, silencing any further words. His tongue danced with mine in an erotic ballet that matched his rhythmic thrusts.

He broke the kiss, trailing kisses down my neck instead. The feeling of his lips on my skin sent shivers down my spine, amplifying the pleasure that was coiling inside of me. "I need... Kaven, please," I gasped out, my words turning into a moan as he increased his pace.

His fingers interlaced with mine, pinning my hands above me on the bed. His other hand was on my hip, guiding our bodies in an intense rhythm that made my breath hitch. The room was filled with the intoxicating scent of sex and desire, and the sounds of our bodies colliding reverberated off the walls.

As if sensing my impending orgasm, Kaven slowed his movements, drawing out the pleasure until I was begging for release. He grinned down at me wickedly before bracing himself on one elbow and sliding his free hand between us. His fingers found my sensitive nub and started circling it in time with his thrusts. The sensation was overwhelming.

Suddenly, I was spiraling into an orgasm so intense it left me breathless. My body convulsed around him, waves of pleasure coursing through me as each thrust sent another wave crashing over me. His name was a mantra on my lips as I writhed beneath him, eyes meeting his in an intimate connection that transcended the physical.

A low groan sounded from his throat in response to my tightening walls. His thrusts became more erratic as he chased his release. An animalistic growl echoed through the room as he climaxed, his body shuddering against mine. The sight of him undone, purely by my effect on him, sent a wave of satisfaction through me that only intensified the afterglow.

He collapsed onto me, panting heavily. We lay there entangled for what seemed like hours, basking in the tranquil intimacy only shared by lovers. His fingers traced lazy patterns on my bare skin, a quiet falling over us.

We lay there content in each other's arms, our bodies slick with sweat and spent passion. Our labored breathing broke the silence of the room, gradually slowing down to normal. Even then, neither of us moved or said anything for what felt like an eternity.

Eventually, Kaven lifted his head from where it lay nestled against my shoulder and his stormy gaze met mine. The intensity of the moment lingered between us, the air thick with unspoken words and emotions.

With a gentle touch, he brushed a lock of hair behind my ear, his fingers lingering against my skin as if trying to convey everything he couldn't voice. I reached up, cupping his face in my hands, feeling the roughness of his stubble beneath my fingertips. I placed a kiss on his lips and laid my head on his chest, not willing to break the moment with words or regret.

The rise and fall of his chest lulled me into sleep and later in the night, when I woke up, he was gone.

14

I needed a moment to breathe, to process everything swirling in my head. The last thing I intended was to complicate things further by having sex with Haddie. But damn, I couldn't stop myself. Being with her was everything I remembered and more. That brought back the irrational anger I had toward her for walking away from me. If she felt the same things I did, it wouldn't have been possible to just up and leave without a word.

To marry some other guy!

Jesus, I was so messed up when it came to Haddie, running in circles knowing the way out but refusing to take it. One minute I was all in to make things right, and the next I changed my mind, doing stupid shit like leaving her in the middle of the night after an incredible round of sex, making it look like I was only using her.

Was it wrong of me to slip away from her room under the cover of darkness?

Unquestionably.

But her presence overpowers me, takes away my control. So, I sent a text to Valley to step in and mounted my bike, racing away from the clubhouse's familiar confines and from Haddie.

"Again?" Fenix's voice intruded upon my restless sleep as I sprawled on his leather couch for the umpteenth time. Groggily, I rubbed my eyes and sat up, feeling the fatigue pull at my bones and the discomfort of sleeping on an unyielding surface clawing at me. With a defeated sigh, I slumped back onto the couch, staring blankly at the ceiling.

"What's eating you?" Fenix asked from the kitchen, where he busied himself brewing coffee. "Ever since you returned from South Carolina, you've been as lost as a hooker in church. Ready to abandon that damned club and join our company?"

"No," I replied curtly. "Not even close. Have you ever been so into a woman that she's all you can see... think of... can't stand to be away from her?"

Fenix paused before joining me in the living area, leaning forward attentively in his chair. "No, never," he admitted. "But it appears you have."

"I met Haddie in South Carolina," I began, unsure of where this confession was leading. "From our very first encounter, I knew she was special. There's something about her that draws me in and chains me to her, and when we... well... it's so fucking good, not like anything I've ever experienced, and damn addicting."

Fenix chuckled at my admission. "So, what's got your wheels spinning?"

As best as I could, I outlined the situation, careful to steer clear of club secrets. Fenix was trustworthy, but some things were better left unsaid. "I'm trying to move past it, to forget, but it gnaws at me that she chose someone else over us, didn't even put up a fight."

Fenix shot back, "Like you're not fighting for the two of you? You're better than this, Kaven. It sounds like Haddie was trapped in a life where she had no control, and yet you choose to wallow in jealousy over hypotheticals."

"I'm resentful of her lack of honesty. Walking away without

uttering a word?"

Fenix sighed heavily. "Talk to her. Listen to her and tell her how you feel. If she is everything you claim, are you willing to let her slip away? The way you encountered her in the woods, her sudden reappearance... if that's not meant to be, I don't know what is."

His words made sense, and I was being a fool. Both he and Valley were right; I needed to reconcile with Haddie, which meant confronting our issues instead of running away like I seemed to always be doing. "I need to get back to the clubhouse."

"Better make it quick before mama catches you or you won't escape until she's stuffed you full," Fenix teased as I headed for the door, acknowledging his accurate prediction with a knowing smile. I jumped onto my bike, the engine's roar echoing the tumultuous emotions inside me. It was time to face Haddie, to hear her out, and finally, stop being a hotheaded asshole.

That's if she'll even talk to me after sneaking out like she was a random one night fuck.

Hadleigh

Valley's unexpected appearance at my door this morning, instead of Kaven, didn't surprise me. Part of me was relieved because I wasn't sure how to face Kaven or what his arrival would mean. I was still grappling with my own feelings, let alone trying to deal with him. His avoidance showed he still wasn't ready to confront our issues, and time was running out before I would be forced to reveal the secret I held.

Was I upset he left me in the middle of the night like a bad afterthought? Yes, but it was my fault for sleeping with him when things were still unresolved. I still don't regret it. Sex with Kaven is so worth it, a feeling I don't think I could ever tire of.

Kick myself the next day, sure, but tire of? Never.

Working with Valley was a welcome change. Unlike the constant tension with Kaven, Valley brought a sense of lightness. As we cleared overgrowth from around the old greenhouse, laughter replaced the usual strain. "You're making me sweat buckets, Hadleigh, and not in the fun way," he joked, pretending to collapse against a tree, sweat streaming down his bare chest.

I paused, wiping sweat from my brow, and chuckled at his theatrics. "Consider this a warm-up for your 'fun activities'," I teased, pointing at a heavy branch that needed to be moved. "Lift me up."

"Think you can handle that?" Valley asked as he hoisted me up, bracing my legs on his stomach. "It might be heavier than you think."

"I'll be careful," I assured him, grabbing the branch. With his arms wrapped around my legs to steady me, I wiggled the branch. It snapped suddenly, throwing me off balance and sending Valley tumbling backward. Instinctively, his arms cradled me, ensuring I landed on him and not on the hard ground.

We lay there momentarily stunned, then burst into laughter when we realized we were unharmed, cushioned by the pile of brush we had cleared. As Valley rolled me to his side, our laughter echoed through the clearing.

Suddenly, Kaven's enraged voice shattered the moment. "You son of a bitch!" he roared, yanking Valley to his feet and delivering a punch to his face before Valley could speak a word.

"Stop!" I screamed, but Kaven ignored me as I scrambled to get up. "It's not what you think!"

Valley stumbled back from Kaven's blow, his hand instinctively rising to his cheek where Kaven's fist had landed. Before either of us could react, Kaven lunged at Valley, tackling him to the ground. They grappled fiercely, fists flying in a blur of motion.

"Stop it, both of you!" I yelled, trying to pull Kaven off Valley, but he was like a man possessed, fueled by anger and hurt.

Valley managed to twist out from under Kaven, scrambling to his feet. "What the fuck!" he shouted, blood trickling from a split lip.

"I warned you!" Kaven snarled, lunging for Valley again, knocking him off his feet, fists flying.

Suddenly, Scotch was there with the man named Harker pulling them apart. "Enough! What the hell's gotten into you two?" Scotch shouted as Kaven struggled against him.

I stepped between them; arms outstretched. "Enough, Kaven! You got this all wrong!"

Kaven hesitated, his chest heaving, fists clenched at his sides. "You're defending him?" he seethed, his voice low and dangerous.

"I'm not defending anyone," I said firmly. "You're misunderstanding the situation."

For a tense moment, Kaven glared at me, his jaw clenched. Then, with a frustrated growl, he turned and stalked away, disappearing into the trees.

I turned to Valley, who was wiping the blood from his lip with the back of his hand. "Are you okay?" I asked, my voice soft with concern.

"Yeah, just a scratch," he said, forcing a smile. "I'll be fine. But you two need to figure this shit out, Hadleigh. Before things get even more out of hand."

"What's this about?" Harked asked, looking between me and Valley.

Scotch looked at me curiously before ordering, "Valley, head back and clean up, and we'll be along."

Valley gave me one last look before nodding and heading down the path. Now that it was over, I felt faint, my head spinning. "Are you okay, Hadleigh?" Ava asked, coming beside me. I didn't even realize she was here. "You look pale."

"Hadleigh?" Harker asked, concerned, as he and Scotch came to stand by my side.

"I'm fine," I managed right before I passed out.

15

THE DEVIL'S HOUSE
West Virginia
Midnight

I was locked and loaded to hash things out with Haddie, set the record straight. But walking in on my best friend tangled up with her? That was a gut punch no one could brace for. I was seeing red, murder on my mind, and the cherry on top? Haddie jumps to his defense. What the hell kind of shit was this?

My head was spinning, chaos crowding my thoughts and making me crazy, so instead of hitting the road like I planned, I pivoted back to confront Haddie. That's when Jonesy blocked my path. "Hold up," he grunted. "Patch called a meeting."

"Damn," I cursed under my breath, trailing Jonesy back inside. I should've smelled trouble the moment Scotch and Harker showed up. I stormed into the clubhouse, my glare fixed on Valley, who was

Midnight

nursing the shiner and busted lip that I gifted him earlier. Felt good seeing him wince in pain.

"Just park it," Harker barked as I brushed past him.

"What the fuck's going on now?" Leather sneered, eyeing Valley and me. "You try to swipe someone else's woman again?"

"Zip it, Leather," Patch cut in, as he, Player, and Scotch filed in and took their seats.

"Spill it. What's this circus with Hadleigh?" Patch demanded, his voice hard as nails.

Valley shot me a look that screamed it was time to come clean. I knew I had to lay it all out because Patch was like a bear with a scent. He knew something.

"It's not what it looked like. This hothead wouldn't hear us out," Valley spats back.

"Are you and Hadleigh sleeping together?" Patch pressed as his stare drilled into me. "Player mentioned you acted mighty familiar with her during the pickup, like you already knew her."

I sighed, my story pouring out for what felt like the millionth time. The shock on their faces morphed into disbelief. "Yeah, you're the one," Patch finally broke the silence, his gaze boring into me. "You're the guy Hadleigh was all torn up about when she talked to Samuel. What are the fucking odds of this shit?"

"What are you getting at?" I asked, my pulse racing.

Patch exhaled slowly. "Clear out, everyone but Scotch, Player, and Midnight." The room emptied, leaving us in a tense huddle. "Scotch and Harker mentioned Hadleigh passed out earlier."

"Passed out?" My concern spiked. "Is she alright?"

Patch leaned in, dropping the bomb. "Midnight, you know if Hadleigh might be pregnant?"

I recoiled, stunned. "No... I mean, she didn't say... Is she?"

"That's still up in the air," Patch admitted. "I put a call into Samuel, who says she told him she could be pregnant, and by the man she had been involved with before being brought back home. After she passed out and came around earlier, Scotch noticed her hand fly to her stomach, scared."

"You wrap it up?" Player chimed in, and my head dropped; no, we hadn't. "I take that as negative."

My mind raced. Haddie had lied to me about being safe, and now she might hide a pregnancy too?

"Listen, Midnight, you need to find out. If my guess is right, she's about three months in and needs to see Doc," Patch advised, his tone concerned. Katherine's recent ordeal hung heavy over us all.

"I'll talk to her," I managed, standing, my legs barely holding me. Haddie might be carrying my baby, and my world was tilting.

"Get back to me tonight. You and Valley still have to answer for this mess," Patch snapped, dismissing me.

I walked out, still in shock at what was just revealed. My future with Haddie was suddenly more complicated than ever.

Hadleigh

"I'm fine, Ava," I reassured her for what felt like the umpteenth time since my fainting episode. The men had all but commanded me to rest in my room, and I attributed my collapse to the sweltering heat. "It's nothing serious."

Ava hesitated before voicing her concern. "Hadleigh, may I ask you something personal?"

"Of course," I responded, bracing myself for the question I knew was coming.

"Are you involved with Midnight? I understand it's supposed to be a cover, but there seems to be a real connection between you two."

I sighed deeply and reclined on the pillow. "Yes, and it's complicated. We met several months ago in South Carolina. I never thought our paths would cross here."

Ava's eyes twinkled with excitement. "I suspected as much! There's an undeniable tension between you two. But how could it be possible, considering your actual purpose here?" She paused thoughtfully before posing another question. "Why do I sense a love-hate dynamic between you two?"

I shrugged nonchalantly, "He struggles with our past and I... well... let's just say things aren't as simple as they appear."

Ava tenderly squeezed my hand. "Real love is never easy, Hadleigh. It often demands navigating through a sea of complications to find your way back to each other. It's a learning process."

That was the crux of it all. I wasn't his true love; merely a temporary distraction from his heartbreak. I knew he cared, but that wasn't enough for me.

"Ava, can I have a word with Haddie alone?" Kaven's voice sounded from the doorway. His unexpected arrival caught us off guard.

"Of course," Ava replied, casting curious glances at us before leaving.

As soon as the door closed behind her, Kaven approached, his gaze intense and searching. The room suddenly felt too small, his presence too close. With no hesitation, he asked, "Haddie, are you pregnant?"

The question struck me like a physical blow, and I stood abruptly, my heart hammering. "Why would you ask that?" I stammered, my voice barely above a whisper.

His hands gripped my arms, his voice a low growl. "Answer me, Haddie. Are you carrying my baby?"

"Yes," I confessed, the truth spilling out, inevitable and terrifying.

He stepped closer, his forehead resting against mine, his eyes searching mine desperately. "And when were you planning to tell me?"

"I... I don't know," I murmured, the admission hollow. "I didn't want you to feel trapped."

His reaction was swift as he moved away, his hand striking the wall, the sound echoing like thunder. "So, never. You were going to marry another man while carrying my baby? How could you, Haddie?"

His accusations stung deeply. He seemed oblivious to the

predicament I was in and the limited power I had over my own life. "How was I supposed to locate you, Kaven? All I had was a first name."

Frustration seethed inside him as he confronted me again. "That doesn't change the fact that you were going to let another man raise my kid without even attempting to find me. You've found me, but still kept silent."

"Kaven, what do you want from me?" I shouted in exasperation as I spread my arms, so frustrated at him for not being willing to see my point of view at all. "Tell me, since you seem to know everything!"

"I want the truth, dammit!" he shouted back, his voice filling the room. "Stop hiding things from me."

"You're one to talk!" I retorted sharply. "As if you aren't keeping things from me and just last night, you snuck away from me like I was a cheap prostitute."

He paused, confusion flickering across his face before he spoke again, softer this time. "I've never lied to you, Haddie, and I'm sorry about last night." His hand moved to rest gently on my stomach. "We need to get married."

A bitter laugh escaped me as I stepped back, my eyes stinging with unshed tears. "As touching as your proposal is, Kaven, the answer is no."

16

**THE DEVIL'S HOUSE
West Virginia
Midnight**

"What do you mean, 'no'?" I asked, my confusion giving way to frustration. "We're having a baby, Haddie," I reminded her, my voice tinged with exasperation.

She drifted towards the window, her back to me, staring out into the afternoon sunlight. "This is exactly why I didn't tell you, Kaven," she murmured, her voice carrying a weight that stopped me in my tracks. "I won't marry a man who is only marrying me because I'm pregnant."

"It's more than that, Haddie," I argued, my voice rising with my temper. "We have something special, and you know it."

Her laughter was sharp, a sound that cut deeper than any words could. She turned, her face covered with hurt. "Something special?" Her voice was a mixture of scorn and sadness. "Kaven, our gardener thinks I'm special too, but that doesn't mean I should marry him. And I certainly won't marry a man who has half the women in this club thinking they're his girlfriends and who's still in love with someone else!" Her accusation was a slap, her words vibrating off the walls as she stormed past me, slamming the door behind her.

"Haddie, wait!" I called out, my plea falling on deaf ears as I hurried after her. "Dammit, Haddie!" My shout was met with the loud bang of the exit door slamming shut.

"Let her go," Harker's voice came from behind me, his hand on my shoulder halting me. "She needs a minute, brother. Give it to her."

"No, Harker," I snapped, shrugging off his grip, my mind racing. "I need to talk to her."

He grabbed my arm, holding me back. "What's gotten into you?" Harker's tone was a mix of concern and reproof. "This isn't like you. You're pushing too hard."

I leaned against the wall, my frustration ebbing out in a heavy sigh. "She drives me crazy," I confessed, rubbing a hand over my face. "She's so damn stubborn."

"And you're not?" Harker challenged; his eyebrow raised in disbelief.

"No, I'm only reacting to what she's done," I said defensively. "She's accusing me of not being honest when I've been nothing but truthful with her."

Harker gave me a skeptical look. "Okay, Midnight, listen up," he said, his expression telling me he wasn't buying my excuses. "Now, I wasn't eavesdropping, just passing by, and I heard what she yelled at you. Have you been messing around with the sweet butts? Does she know about Aislynn? Because I guarantee you, she's heard about that fiasco."

I froze, the reality of his words hitting me hard. I hadn't clarified that I wasn't involved with the sweet butts, and I never thought about her hearing the rumors about Aislynn. "Is she right? Are you still hung up on Aislynn?"

"No, and no," I insisted, my frustration growing. "I sorted that out before I came back here. Once I met Haddie, everything changed."

"Then let her cool off, and talk to her," Harker advised, clapping me on the shoulder. "Then sit her down and explain everything that's going on inside you. You can't blame her for not wanting to settle down with a guy who she thinks loves playing around while trying to forget another woman. And that, my brother, is exactly what she's thinking."

I nodded slowly, his words sinking in. "I'm just messing this all up, and you're not the first person to tell me, but when I'm around Haddie...it's different with her."

"That's how it should feel if she's the right one," Harker said, a smile flickering across his face as he walked away. "Give her some time."

I nodded, leaning back against the wall, trying to muster patience —a virtue I was sorely lacking at the moment.

"Midnight?" Aislynn's voice pulled me from my thoughts. I turned to find her standing there, a look of uncertainty clouding her features.

"Are you okay?" I asked, my eyes briefly scanning the hallway for any sign of trouble, meaning Leather.

"It's okay. Braden is at the garage. He dropped me off to visit Katherine," she assured me, stepping closer. "I saw Hadleigh when I was coming in. Is everything okay?"

My eyes unintentionally drifted to her rounded stomach, imagining what Haddie might look like in a few months. Meeting Aislynn's gaze, I caught the unspoken question there. "They will be," I replied, suddenly aware of how it might look with me staring.

"Midnight, I'm happy to see you find somebody," Aislynn said, moving closer. "I felt so bad after everything you did for me and you leaving..."

"I'll admit, at first it was tough. I wanted to be the one to help you, to heal you. While I was away, I realized it was something in my past pushing me toward you, the need to atone for something else dogging me."

"You helped me when I needed it," she assured me. "And I'm so grateful."

"That's good, and I don't regret what happened. It led me to Haddie, and I wouldn't change that for anything," I said, my voice firm and sincere.

She hugged me, a gentle embrace that spoke volumes. "That makes me so happy, Midnight, and relieves a lot of my guilt."

I returned the hug and gently pushed her away; the contact affirming what I felt—or didn't feel—for her. "No guilt, Aislynn. I care about you and only want to see you happy and thriving," I told her, a smile on my lips. "Now, since I value my life, go find Katherine before Leather shows up and buries me out in the back."

As she walked away, Aislynn's laughter followed her down the hallway at the thought of Leather's reaction. The back door opened, and Valley appeared, his face tense. "I just directed Ry where to drop that lumber you had him pick up for Hadleigh's greenhouse."

"Okay, I'll go—" I started, but Valley cut me off.

"No, you won't," he said sharply. "Patch wants us in his office. My fear came true and this shit with you and Hadleigh is blowing back on me."

I took one last look at the door Haddie had exited through, sighed, and followed Valley, hoping the distraction would give Haddie the space she needed—and me the clarity to fix what I'd broken.

Hadleigh

I rounded the corner, making a wide circle to throw Kaven off my trail, hoping he'd head toward the greenhouse. My chest heaved with each breath, and the adrenaline pumping through my veins was almost too much to handle. A few moments to compose myself was what I needed before facing him again. My pulse pounded in my ears as I paused, straining to hear any sign of pursuit. Kaven's voice floated down the hallway, clear and resonant. "I wouldn't change it for anything." A woman's soft reply followed, and the voice was unmistakable.

I froze.

My heart thundered in my chest, each beat so loud I feared it would give me away. Peeking around the corner, I saw them—Kaven and Aislynn—in an embrace, their bodies so close it made my stomach churn. A pain like I had never known tore through me, stealing my breath and making me dizzy. Oh god, he loved her still, and this was the proof. It was like a knife twisting in my gut, each twist deeper and more excruciating than the last. I turned and fled, my movements automatic, my mind a whirl of agony. How would I survive this? I could only tell myself to be strong so many times before my heart bled out, leaving me shattered on the ground.

I ran toward the greenhouse, desperate to escape, suffocating under the weight of my realization and the mistakes I had made. My lungs burned, and my legs felt like lead, but I couldn't stop. The image of them together was seared into my mind, a relentless torment. My feet skidded to a halt when I saw a big black truck parked along the path. The vehicle seemed out of place, standing out in the familiar surroundings. Slowing, I scanned the area and spotted a man unloading lumber. He must be delivering the wood I needed.

As I took in the open door of his truck, a reckless thought took root. A way out—away from the pain and Kaven. My heart raced even faster at the idea of running. I was willing to risk it, to leave everything behind. I had friends from college who might help, at least for a little while, or at least I hoped. The urge to escape, to flee from the unbearable heartache, was overwhelming.

Ensuring I wasn't being watched, I slipped into the truck's back seat, pulling a blanket over myself. My body trembled as I settled into the cramped space, my nerves electric. Every sound seemed amplified—the rustle of the blanket, the distant hum of machinery, the approaching footsteps. I heard the man shut the tailgate and climb into the driver's seat, the seatbelt clicking as the truck roared to life. The vibration of the engine felt like an earthquake beneath me, shaking me to my core.

Oh god, was I really doing this? It was impulsive and insane, but the thought of facing Kaven was far more terrifying than the unknown. The truck stopped at the gate, then moved again. Each jolt of the vehicle made my heart leap into my throat. The man's phone rang, and he answered, "Yeah." He was silent for a moment, then said, "I'll be there in a few and take a look at it."

Finally, the road smoothed out, and I knew we were on the highway. The steady hum of tires on pavement was almost soothing, a contrast to the turmoil inside me. My heart began to calm, the pounding in my ears subsiding just in time to hear a deep voice chuckle, "You can come out of hiding now. Climb up here and tell me what's got you running from that clubhouse."

17

Hadleigh

The shock of his words paralyzed me for a moment, rendering me speechless. Crap, he knew I was here the whole time! My breath caught in my throat as I processed what he had said. Slowly, I pulled the blanket off and peered over the seat, meeting his steady gaze in the rearview mirror. His dark eyes held no malice, just curiosity and a hint of amusement. It must be my imagination playing tricks on me, but he looked a lot like Kaven. With a shaky breath, I uncurled myself from the back seat, my hands trembling a little from being caught.

"Why didn't you say anything if you knew I was here?" I asked, climbing into the front seat and eyeing him suspiciously. "You're not some serial killer, are you? Because that would be just my luck."

"Can't say I am," he laughed, introducing himself. "Name's Ry.

You're safe with me."

"Hadleigh," I replied, my voice barely above a whisper.

"Okay, Hadleigh, what's going on?" he asked, his tone softening.

"I just needed a ride into town," I said, looking out the window, giving him only a half-truth.

"Why not just ask? You act like you're escaping... are you?" His eyes flicked to me and back to the road.

I sighed, leaning my head against the seat. "It's complicated, and I can't go into all of it. But I wasn't being held against my will, if that's what you're thinking."

"That's exactly what I'm thinking," he said, his voice tinged with concern. "So, if that's not the case, why are you running?"

"Because Kaven—" I stopped, realizing I was about to spill my private business to a stranger. "I just want to move on."

He looked surprised, then thoughtful. "So, I take it Kaven is your boyfriend, and he did something to piss you off."

"Like I said, it's complicated. If you could just take me to the bus station or something, that would be great."

"You don't even have a phone or money on you. You won't get very far," he stated, his eyes sliding over to me. "How about I take you back to my place until you figure things out?" He leaned over, reaching into the glove box, and handed me a small handgun. "It's loaded. It'll give you peace of mind that I'm not going to hurt you."

I felt the heavy metal in my hand and checked it to make sure he wasn't lying. "Okay," I said, sticking it in my pocket, since I had no better options.

"You seem familiar with that," he smirked.

"My grandfather taught me early how to protect myself, if need be," I informed him, smiling at the memory.

"Smart," he replied, returning my smile. Again, a feeling of familiarity washed over me, but I shook it off. He pulled into the parking lot of an apartment building and said, "Come inside, and don't be surprised if my brothers notice you and ask questions. They're a nosy bunch."

"You guys live together?"

"No, we all have our own apartments, all on the same floor so we can look after our mama," Ry said, holding the door open for me and then leading me down the hallway into his apartment. Before my eyes could even scan the apartment, a knock sounded, and two other men entered. I immediately knew they were Ry's brothers. And again, I thought of Kaven.

"Hey, Ry," one said, looking me over with curiosity. "Saw you come in and thought we'd stop by and meet your lady friend."

"Hadleigh, this is Fenix and Grey," Ry introduced me, giving them a long look. "She hitched a ride from the clubhouse."

Fenix raised an eyebrow in surprise. If I didn't know better, I'd swear he recognized me. "Really? How'd you end up here?"

"Like I told your brother, it's complicated, but he's helping me out."

"Yeah, she's having problems with her boyfriend, Kaven," Ry said, and something passed between the men. "And I told her she could crash here until she figures things out."

Grey looked me over. "You're lucky you ran into Ry. Surely you weren't planning on traipsing around with only the clothes on your back?"

Before I could answer, another knock sounded, and another man entered, also looking eerily similar to Kaven. "Hey Ry, heard you brought a woman to your apartment," he smirked, his eyes finding me and unabashedly looking me over. "A redhead, you surprise me."

"It's not like that, Cam," Ry and Fenix snapped in unison.

I looked between the men, realizing this was no coincidence; the resemblance was too strong, and the knowing looks between them triggered memories of past conversations with Kaven about his family, and his five brothers. My eyes widened. "You're Kaven's brothers!"

"And thank God it was Ry you pulled this stunt with," Kaven's angry voice came from the doorway. "Anything could have happened to you! What the hell were you thinking?"

The Devil's House: West Virginia Midnight

I had been going out of my mind looking for her. After Patch tore Valley and me a new asshole for keeping my relationship with Haddie a secret, I frantically searched everywhere, but she was nowhere to be found. Just as I was about to start combing the woods, a text came in from Ry: he'd found a red-headed stray in his truck and taken her home.

"You ratted me out!" Haddie screamed, spinning around to confront Ry, pulling a gun from her pocket. "I'm not going back!"

Ry held up his hands in defense, a nervous laugh escaping. "No need to get violent, Hadleigh. You can put the gun away. If you don't want to go back, nobody here will make you."

Why in the hell did she have a gun?

I reached Haddie and yanked the gun from her hand, her scream of outrage cutting through me as I tossed it to Ry. "What do you mean you're not coming back? Why the hell did you run in the first place?"

"I'm not some prisoner. I can do what I want," she spat, her eyes blazing. "I want to start my life over, on my own terms."

"All this because I said we needed to get married?" I asked, feeling the ground shift beneath me at her attitude. "I know we have some misunderstandings to clear up, but isn't this extreme? And you do realize there's a reason you're in hiding? Don't be stupid."

"Don't call me stupid!" she shouted, tears beginning to stream down her face. "And I don't think we have any misunderstandings to clear up. Things are clear as day, and I understand everything completely!"

"Haddie, quit being stubborn and calm down!" I reached for her, concerned at how upset she was, but she jerked back and out of reach.

She jabbed her finger at me. "Listen carefully, Kaven. I will not marry you just because I'm pregnant with your baby!"

A shocked gasp from behind us reminded us we weren't alone. We turned to see Mama rushing over to Haddie. "My Kaven is going to have a baby?" she exclaimed, wrapping Haddie in a tight embrace and kissing her cheek. "Come, you need to calm down and eat. This isn't good for the little one."

"I..." Haddie stuttered as Mama led her from the room, a bewildered look on her face.

"This is the most interesting thing to happen in a long time," Cam chuckled, his eyes gleaming. "Little Bro, the first to become a daddy and making Mama's dream come true."

"Yeah, I never saw this coming," Ry laughed, shaking his head at me. "What the hell did you do to her to cause her to act this way?"

"Did she catch you with someone else? One of those women you guys keep around that clubhouse?" Bo smirked. Still bitter over Sarah, he won't stop bashing the club, and I'm damn sick of it.

"Shut your mouth, Bo. You don't know what you're talking about!" I snarled, fury rising in me. "This is not your business."

"Did she?" Cam asked cautiously. "I mean, shit, your girl tried running from you. That's not normal and usually means you cheated."

"Really Cam? You should know me better than that. What the fuck?" I snarled, getting even more pissed off by the minute.

"Hey, we're just trying to figure out what the hell is going on, and it's no secret you like the ladies," Cam shot back, defending himself.

"I think things have changed," Fenix said, watching me thoughtfully.

"Okay, let's stop the bickering and talk about this later. We should probably go save Hadleigh before Mama stuffs her fuller than a Thanksgiving turkey," Grey said, and he was right. Mama had been after us to get married and start families for years, and with Haddie being the first, she's going to get the overloaded version of Mama's attention.

I'm still reeling from her running away. It's still dangerous for her, and I needed to get answers so this wouldn't happen again. She was carrying my baby, and I didn't take that lightly. Now I had two lives that meant everything to me to protect.

18

Hadleigh

What was happening? How did I end up sitting in Kaven's mother's kitchen being fed like a stray cat taken in from the cold? Fate has a twisted sense of humor, always dangling a carrot just to whack me with a stick. "Here, sweetie, drink this. It's calming," Mrs. Rafferty said, placing a steaming cup of tea in front of me.

I took a cautious sip and sighed. "Thank you, Mrs. Rafferty."

"Call me Mama, we're family now," she replied with a warm smile, and the fact was she was a petite woman, and still beautiful for her age, it just didn't feel right calling her Mama. She bustled around the kitchen like a whirlwind, throwing ingredients into bowls with the precision of a seasoned chef. "I hope you like stuffed peppers and almond cake."

"Umm, I've never had either," I admitted, taking another sip of the surprisingly delicious tea. It really was calming me down.

She stopped mid-step, surprise lighting up her face. "You've never had stuffed peppers or almond cake? Are you of the Irish or Scottish?" she asked, eyeing my red hair with curiosity.

I chuckled, "Believe it or not, I'm Italian."

She beamed at me, her eyes twinkling. "Hair so red, I wouldn't have guessed. Your name is Hadleigh, yes?" I nodded, and she pressed on. "Now, tell me why you don't want to marry my son?"

I shrugged, struggling to find the words until I finally managed, "I want him to want me because he loves me, not just see me as an obligation."

"He loves you, that's plain to see. I see the fire in his eyes when you two argue," she said, waving a spoon at me like a magic wand. "Kaven was always the most sensitive and passionate of my boys. I'm guessing he fell hard quickly and isn't handling it well. But you two have something I can see it, a passion that all young lovers should have," she said, with an almost wistful look in her eyes.

"Mama, you did not just use the word 'lovers'," Fenix said, feigning horror as all the men filed into the room. Kaven sat next to me, his eyes filled with questions.

"Your mama was a young girl once. How do you think you boys were made?" she challenged him with a mischievous smile and a wink at me before turning back to the stove.

"We eat and then head back to the clubhouse," Kaven whispered, leaning close. "You took a big risk being seen by leaving, and I'll be lucky if Patch doesn't find out about this and kills me."

I bit back a retort, not wanting to cause a scene in front of his sweet mother. Besides, the sight of his brothers watching us with amused smiles was enough to keep me quiet. They all looked so much alike, the only differences being age and Fenix's sea-green eyes instead of black. The family resemblance was uncanny.

For the next hour, I indulged in delicious food and listened to the men's banter. Mama Rafferty kept piling food onto our plates with a smile, and I found it oddly comforting. This kind of warmth and togetherness was foreign to me. My family loved me, but displays of affection were rare, and we never sat around the table talking and laughing like this.

Finally, when I thought I couldn't eat another bite without bursting, Kaven announced it was time to leave. His mother hugged me, patting my stomach as she looked at Kaven. "I want you to bring Hadleigh for Sunday supper."

"I will, Mama," he promised, kissing her cheek. "Love you, see you Sunday."

As we walked to the exit, Kaven tried to take my hand, but I shook it off. "Haddie, what is wrong? I know you're pissed, but goddammit!"

I knew I was acting childish, but I couldn't help it. The hurt was too deep, so I gave him the silent treatment. He just shook his head and stopped me at the door. "Keep your head lowered and lean into me so you won't be recognized," he ordered, pulling me against his side with a grip I couldn't escape.

At his motorcycle, he pulled out a helmet and plopped it onto my head, fastening it for me like a child since I was acting like one. He straddled the bike and said, "Climb on."

With a huff, I climbed on behind him, gingerly touching his sides like he was covered in poison. He kickstarted the bike and lurched forward, causing me to screech in terror, my arms flying around his waist to hold on for dear life.

"Hold on tight," Kaven called over the roar of the engine, his voice filled with amusement. He revved the engine, and we shot down the road like a bullet.

The world blurred around us as we sped through the streets, the wind whipping against my face. My initial terror began to morph into exhilaration as the motorcycle leaned into the curves, Kaven expertly navigating the twists and turns. The city flickered past us in a dizzying display, and I found myself clinging to him not just out of necessity, but out of a strange sense of trust and excitement.

Kaven's body was warm and solid against mine, his confidence clear. He glanced back at me briefly, a mischievous grin on his face. "Having fun yet?"

"Terrified, but yes!" I shouted back, unable to suppress a laugh. The thrill of the ride was starting to get to me, my fear replaced by a rush of adrenaline.

We zoomed through the city, the bike weaving effortlessly through traffic. Kaven took us onto the open highway, the landscape constantly shifting. The ride was wild and reckless, and I couldn't help but feel alive in a way I hadn't in a long time.

Kaven slowed down, guiding the bike onto the winding country road that led to the clubhouse. The evening air was cool and fresh, filled with the scent of blooming flowers and earth, as he pulled to a stop.

He turned off the engine, the sudden silence almost deafening after the roar of the ride. "What did you think?" he asked, his eyes sparkling with excitement.

I pulled off the helmet, my hair a wild mess. "That was... incredible," I admitted, my heart still pounding. "It was so exhilarating and nothing like riding my bike."

Kaven's expression softened, and he reached out to tuck a stray strand of hair behind my ear. "I'm glad," he said quietly. "I wanted to cheer you up, see you smile and laugh."

For a moment, I felt a flicker of hope. Maybe things could be different, and we could work through all our problems. "Thank you, Kaven," I said, my voice sincere.

He smiled; a genuine, heart-stopping smile that made my stomach do a flip and my thighs clench with need. Our eyes were locked as his hand moved toward my face and my heart sped up with anticipation.

But just as quickly, that feeling was extinguished by the sound of a high-pitched female voice. My heart dropped as I turned to see a curvy brunette approaching us. Her high heels making her wobbly as she made her way over to where we stood.

Hope shattered in the span of only seconds.

Kaven's smile disappeared and his hand froze mid-air as she came to stand in front of us. "Finally, I came tonight just to see you, baby," she cooed, her attention solely focused on Kaven. "Valley said he didn't know when you'd be back."

My blood boiled as she casually looked me up and down with detached curiosity. "Oh, am I interrupting?"

Before I could even respond, Kaven, whose eyes never left mine, snapped at her, "I'm busy."

But she wasn't deterred as she suggested, "Darn, I was hoping you didn't already have a girl for the night, but we can share," she insisted, her hand now on my arm. "Midnight can handle both of us, right, baby?"

The rage bubbled inside me as I finally found my voice. "No thanks. You can have him all to yourself," I spat, before storming away.

Kaven called after me, but I refused to stop and talk. I practically ran through the common room and down the hallway until I reached my room. Slamming the door shut and flipping the lock, I leaned against it and caught my breath.

But my peace was short-lived as I heard Kaven pounding on the other side of the door. "Dammit, Haddie!" he shouted. "I didn't invite that bitch here and you know it. We need to talk and work this shit out!"

Frustration and hurt mingled within me as I walked over to the connecting door and flipped the lock just as Kaven's hand touched the knob from his side. "Stop, Haddie!" he yelled, still pounding on the door. "Stop running from me and talk to me, for fuck's sake!"

But I didn't want to talk about it. Everything was always an illusion meant to fool me and I was so tired of starring in the magic show. So, I leaned my forehead against the cool wood of the door, trying to ignore his desperate pleas.

Tears streamed down my face as I leaned against the door, my heart aching at the realization that our relationship will never be what it was by that waterfall in South Carolina. *You're nothing but a stupid dreamer, Hadleigh.*

My fist hit the wall with a loud thud, skin splitting and leaving a bloody print. Was I being punished? Shit, I didn't even know who the hell that bitch was or why she showed up acting like I was a tomcat prowling the night, just as I was making a breakthrough with Haddie. Yes, I had a history of messing around, but I've changed over the last year. The party life wasn't as appealing, and since I've been with Haddie, no other woman could take her place.

Surely, she could see that we needed to talk this out. All the misunderstandings needed to be worked through, and we couldn't do that by constantly fighting. I stormed out of my room and back into the common room, dropping onto a stool and signaling Adam for a beer.

"Looks like you got woman problems," Lucky chuckled from the stool next to me. "Those redheads can be a hot-headed bunch, but if you can tame one of 'em? Lordy, the time you'll have."

I only grunted in reply, taking a long drink of my beer. I glanced at my bloody knuckles, the fresh crimson stark against my calloused skin. Another mark to add to my collection. My thoughts drifted back to Haddie again. Her fire red hair and dancing blue eyes now held enough anger to light up the whole damn clubhouse.

The music pumped from the speakers, a fierce rhythm of heavy metal that churned the air and set pulses racing and ears ringing. I casually glanced around the room as laughter rang over the music, mingling with the crack of pool balls being struck and the clink of bottles.

I glanced at Lucky, a scar-riddled bear of a man who'd long passed his prime but had more stories than anyone I knew. He took another swig from his bottle and gave me a grin. "She'll come around," he assured me with a knowing smile.

"I didn't think it would be this hard," I mumbled into my bottle.

"Welcome to reality, kid."

"Midnight?" a female voice said from behind me, and I turned to see the woman from outside. "I didn't mean to cause problems, but it seems she left you alone and, well..." Her fingers traced a path down her chest provocatively.

My eyes flicked up and down, taking her in, trying for the life of me to remember her. Jesus, I must have been drunk that night. She was attractive in a stiletto-and-tight-dress kind of way, but there were thousands like her floating in and out of here all year long.

Forgettable.

She lacked the fire in her eyes that Haddie had, the spark of intelligence that always impressed me. Haddie was so damn unique and beautiful it twisted my gut thinking about it. The woman in front of me lacked the familiar tug at my heartstrings, the binding ties that never seem to come undone, only getting tighter.

I cut her off with a glare when her hand reached for me. "Don't," I grumbled, tilting my bottle back for another swallow. "I just want to drink my beer... alone."

"But, I..." she started, but Lucky interrupted her with a hearty chuckle.

"He's made his choice," he croaked out, slapping my shoulder hard. "All you're doin' is makin' a fool of yourself, honey."

She huffed and walked away, leaving me to my beer and brooding. The music thumped on, each beat resonating in my chest like the anger and confusion pulsing through my veins.

"Women," Lucky spoke, finishing his bottle and burping loudly. He motioned to Adam for another round. "They'll spin you 'round, that's for sure."

I couldn't help but chuckle at his words. "Isn't that the truth?" I mumbled, tracing patterns on the bar with my finger.

Lucky looked at his watch and said, "I better go check on Mikie. Promised Sarah I'd look out for him while she works. The kid's got the hots for Ava and tends to overstay his welcome at the barn."

"Typical teenager. We've all been there." I chuckled at the image of Scotch tolerating Mikie tailing behind Ava. "I didn't think Sarah would still work at the club?"

"Where you been, boy?" Lucky asked. "Jonesy is quittin', Snipe is takin' over. She's just helpin' out while Jonesy trains Snipe."

"I should have seen that coming."

"Yep, a strip club ain't no place for a taken man, especially if that man is engaged to my daughter," Lucky smirked, getting up and heading out.

I didn't see the appeal of a strip club that most men did, and they always act like they struck gold when they walked inside. When most of them had a good woman at home waiting for them, just plain stupid.

Alcohol and lighting hid so much shit and after working there, you see the back end—the women, some drug addicts, some dancing to survive financially, and some just running from a past of abuse, their smiles disappearing as soon as the music ends, and the lights go out. And the look on some of the men's faces, predatory and sick, always reminded me of the day me and Valley found my sister Kezia, beaten and raped before someone threw her away like trash.

Shit like that stays with you forever, the image imprinted on your brain.

But my mama always taught me a kind word with a smile can go a long way, and I always tried to do that throughout my life and found myself doing it a lot at Twisted Heat. I looked at the time on my phone and stood. Duty called, and I needed to get moving.

19

Hadleigh

I had done nothing but toss and turn, unable to sleep, my thoughts consumed with my situation and how to handle it. So far, I'm doing nothing but making a mess of it. My grandfather always said I was impulsive and needed to think things through before running headfirst into something.

But did I listen?

Flipping the covers off, I got out of bed and walked to the window, staring out into the night, my eyes drawn to the sky. Here, unlike my home in Philadelphia, the sky was so clear, the stars so bright, with no city lights to taint it. I loved it and could look at it forever and the nature surrounding me; it was spectacular with all the mountains. I was itching to explore every single inch of it.

A walk. That's what I need—a walk to calm my mind, and then maybe I could get some sleep. I worried about my baby and what all this stress was causing; I needed to be more mindful of my pregnancy. Going to the dresser to grab something to wear, I stopped in my tracks as I heard a giggle coming from Kaven's room.

Surely, I heard wrong. He wouldn't bring a woman right next door to me, would he? With my heart in my stomach, I moved to the door that separated our rooms, putting my ear against the cool wood. "You like that, don't you, baby?" a woman's voice purred.

My hurt turned into blood-red rage at the sounds I heard that could only mean one thing, after telling me I was wrong, and he wanted to work things out! I was going to kill him!

So, without hesitating, I threw the door open with a bang and marched into the room snarling, "You got one hell of a nerve—"

"What the hell, Hadleigh?" Valley shouted, as the naked woman kneeling on the floor in front of him screeched and fell backward.

I threw my hand over my mouth in horror at my mistake as Valley stood in front of me with a shocked expression on his face, the girl on the floor looking at me like I was crazy as she scrambled to her feet and grabbed her clothes, probably thinking I was some deranged girlfriend.

My feet backed slowly toward the door with an apologetic smile on my face. "I'm sorry, Valley, I thought..." I mumbled in embarrassment, my eyes going where they shouldn't, raising an eyebrow and thinking all men were not the same.

Seeing the focus of my eyes, he realized what I was seeing. "Holy hell, Midnight is going to kill me!" he growled and moved toward the bed, grabbing a blanket.

I took a step back, my mind racing. "Umm, see you tomorrow?" I said before hurrying into my room and slamming the door shut, leaning against it and looking up at the ceiling, my face beet red with embarrassment. Okay, that was going to make things awkward with Valley the next time I saw him.

The silence in my room felt deafening. My pulse pounded in my ears as I slid down to the floor, hugging my knees. "What just happened?" I whispered to myself, half laughing, half crying. My mind pictured the look on Valley's face, a mix of surprise and something else —was that amusement?

I couldn't help but giggle despite my mortification. "Way to go, Hadleigh," I muttered. "Walking into a scene right out of a bad comedy." I thought about Valley's expression again, and the giggle turned into a laugh. The more I thought about it, the funnier it seemed, until I was laughing so hard I had to put my hand over my mouth to muffle the sound.

The laughter was cathartic, a release of all the pent-up tension. When I finally calmed down, I felt lighter, almost giddy. I knew things would be awkward with Valley, but maybe this ridiculous moment was what I needed to settle my mind for a bit. Maybe tomorrow I'd find a way to laugh about it with him.

I climbed back into bed, a smile playing on my lips. For the first time in days, I felt like I might actually get some sleep. It's amazing what laughter can do for the soul, no matter how embarrassing.

Damn, I was tired. I hated guarding the gate all night, but Patch had laid down mine and Valley's punishment and we were damn lucky it wasn't a beating and only grunt work. Valley and I had worked out he would take the day and I would take the night since I didn't want him spending time with Haddie.

Just as the sun rose from behind the mountains, I saw Valley heading toward the gatehouse and I walked out to meet him, ready to get inside and find Haddie so we could talk. "Thanks for telling your girl that you had gate duty," he snapped as he got closer.

"Why? What happened?"

"It's going to piss you off," he warned me.

"Just tell me what fucking happened," I snapped, already getting mad, and I hadn't even heard the story yet.

"I brought Tracy back to the room for a late night special and Hadleigh busted into the room just when it was getting good, thinking it was you in the room," he informed me.

My jaw tightened at the implication of what he just told me. "What exactly did she see?"

"This isn't my fault," he argued, telling me all I needed to know. "I wasn't exactly expecting company!"

"She saw you naked?" I bit out, jealousy making me want to kill him where he stood. He was already on thin ice with me over Haddie.

"How could I have avoided it?"

"By locking the goddamned door before starting your bedtime special!" I snarled. "Or how about not bringing a woman back to your room to fuck when you're supposed to be looking out for Haddie?"

"Listen, man, it happened, and you need to get over it," he said, moving around me. "And for the sake of my sanity and our friendship, will you figure this shit out with her?"

"She's pregnant," I murmured at his back.

He turned on his heel, his face shocked. "What did you say?"

"She's going to have my baby," I replied, running my hand down my face. "She's known about the pregnancy for months and said nothing and, to top it off, she's refusing to marry me."

Valley leaned against the gatehouse, still stunned. "Wow, how'd it happen? I mean, I know how it happened, but you're not one to risk getting a woman knocked up. You sure it's yours?"

"It's mine, I don't doubt it, and she just makes me get carried away and nothing else matters when I'm with her," I admitted. "And the cherry on top... My brothers and Mama know."

"Yesterday?" he asked, eyebrow raised, and I nodded. "Mama is over the moon, I bet."

"Yeah, I haven't seen her that happy since before Kezia died."

"That about killed her," Valley said, looking thoughtful. "About killed me too." Valley and Kezia were dating, and he's never gotten over her death. I don't think Valley will ever commit to anyone. His heart died right along with my sister. Valley gave himself a shake and asked, "So daddy, how are you going to make her come around and commit to you?"

"That, my brother, is a good question. Haddie is hard-headed and getting her to listen isn't easy," I chuckled, to lighten the mood.

Valley laughed and said, "If you could see how pissed off she was last night, man, she was fit to kill. She wants you, brother, that's for sure."

"I'll admit I like that temper of hers and I plan on making good use of it later on." My eyes looked toward the clubhouse. "I'm gonna go get Haddie and have some coffee before I fall asleep on my feet."

As I started up the hill, Valley called behind me. "I hope everything works out for you two, and soon."

I threw my hand up in answer and kept walking, the very same hope in my mind.

20

Hadleigh

I had just slipped on my sandals when a knock sounded on the door. I knew Kaven was here to escort me to breakfast, though it wasn't really necessary—I wasn't getting kidnapped on my way to the kitchen. Despite the child that now connected us, I still wasn't ready to talk about our relationship, or lack thereof.

When I opened the door, my eyes widened in surprise at the sight of Ava and a teenage boy standing there, both smiling. "Morning, Hadleigh. Patch needs to talk to you in his office."

"Ahh, sure," I replied, confused as to why he wanted to see me so early and the reason behind it.

"This way," Ava said, leading me down the hall. "This is Mikie, by the way."

"You've got the reddest hair I've ever seen," Mikie observed, falling into step beside me. "Hear you're Midnight's girl. I know his brother Bo." Ava shot him a scolding glance over her shoulder, prompting him to add, "I don't mean it in a bad way about your hair. It's just different, is all."

"Yeah, my hair could guide a lost traveler at night," I chuckled at his honesty.

"Here we are," Ava said, stopping in front of a door and knocking lightly. Player opened it and signaled me inside. My eyes caught Kaven's from where he was seated in a chair by the wall.

"Have a seat," Patch ordered, pointing to the chair beside Kaven.

I took the seat and asked, "What's going on?"

Before anyone could reply, the door opened, and Samuel strolled into the room. Why was he here? I felt Kaven stiffen beside me as Samuel greeted me. "Hello, Hadleigh," he said, taking a seat beside Player.

"So, what's this about?" Patch asked, leaning forward, his arms on the desk.

"We seem to have a problem," Samuel said, his cold eyes locking onto mine. "Did you tell anyone about the plan?"

"Not a soul," I replied, confused. "Why are you asking me this?"

"Because I believe I'm being followed," he informed the room. "So again, Hadleigh, did you tell anyone?"

"She said she didn't, and anyone could be following you, given the business you're in," Kaven snapped, speaking up for me.

Samuel's eyes flashed with irritation at Kaven before he said, "I'm going to let that slide since you're her boyfriend, and I understand your need to defend and protect, but tread lightly, boy."

"I'll say whatever—" Kaven began, but Patch cut him off with a glare.

"Shut it. Get on with it, Samuel. Tell us what you want."

"If there's even a chance I'm being followed, it's only a matter of time before Hadleigh is located here," Samuel said, his voice urgent as he looked at me. "Not only that, but your grandfather is offering a five-million-dollar reward for your safe return. The poster will hit the underground tomorrow."

Player whistled. "Shit, that'll bring out the hunters."

"Exactly," Samuel replied. "Hadleigh needs to be moved fast, somewhere remote."

"I can take her to my cabin," Kaven suggested. "It's in the middle of the wilderness, not easily accessible."

"The one you took Aislynn to when you hid her?" Player asked, raising an eyebrow.

Immediately, I didn't want to go there—not where he had a history with the woman he loved. "Are there other options?" I asked, my eyes pleading.

Kaven turned to me, his voice tense. "What's your problem, Haddie? Would you rather be taken back and marry Samuel?"

"He's right, Hadleigh," Samuel agreed. "Not enough time has passed. I thought you wanted to be with this man, and I understand you're carrying his child."

Kaven's eyes bored into me like lasers, and the other men watched, waiting for my reply. I knew I couldn't fight going to that cabin without revealing my reasons, so I caved. "Fine, how much longer will I have to hide?" I asked Samuel.

He sighed, thinking for a moment. "Another month should do it. I want to ensure your pregnancy progresses to a point where your grandfather has to accept it. I can then assure him there are no hard feelings when we break the contract."

"What do you mean, 'accept it'? What's he gonna do?" Kaven snarled.

"In our world, inconveniences are taken care of," Samuel said, his voice cold and detached. "Her grandfather isn't going to break a contract with a powerful man like me just so Hadleigh can have a biker's baby."

"That's fucked up," Kaven shot back. "And these people claim to love her? Trust me, she won't be coming back to the likes of you and them."

Seeing Samuel's face turn red, I grabbed Kaven's hand, giving it a squeeze. "Let it go," I whispered nervously. "Let's just get ready to leave for your cabin."

"Midnight, take Hadleigh to get some breakfast, then gather any supplies you'll need from around the clubhouse. You can use my bike's pull-behind trailer," Patch ordered, clearly done with the conversation. "I want you on the road in two hours."

"We'll be in touch," Samuel told me as I let Kaven guide me out of the room. Samuel was not a man to play with, and I didn't want Kaven saying anything else.

Outside the room, Kaven cornered me against the wall. "How could you even think of letting a man like that raise my kid?" he snarled, his eyes searching mine. "How, Haddie?"

The Devil's House — West Virginia Midnight

Her hands slammed against my chest, trying to push me away, but I was immovable. "You're being unfair and not trying to understand the situation I was in," she shot back, her eyes blazing with anger.

"Was it because he was rich? You thought that would make up for that block of ice raising a kid that wasn't his? Or did you find him a better option than a guy like me?"

"Do you hear yourself?" she snarled, shoving my chest again. "I'm so sick of you accusing me of things you know nothing about!"

I knew I was blowing it again, but the jealousy was eating me alive, gnawing at me with the knowledge of what Samuel said about taking care of inconveniences. Who the fuck talked about babies that way? "You would have let them take care of your inconvenience?"

"How could you say something like that!" she cried, tears welling in her eyes as she gave a hard shove, slipping under my arm and heading for the back door.

I was hot on her heels, the volatile emotions inside me boiling over. I ran after her and cornered her against the building. "Let me go," she whispered furiously through her tears.

"No, not until you tell me the truth! Would you have let them kill our baby?" I pressed her, my forehead dropping against hers, my breathing heavy from all the emotions surging through me.

"Never!" she shouted, her fists balling against my chest. "I would never have allowed that, and I can't believe you would think so lowly of me."

Before I could react, she brought her knee up, hitting me square in the nuts, and I dropped to my knees in pain. "What the fuck!" I groaned, looking up at her.

"I'll meet you out front in a few hours," she shouted, turning on her heel and fleeing back into the clubhouse. How could such a small woman cause so much pain?

I heard clapping and looked up to see Samuel and Patch laughing at me. "You deserve that pain," Patch chuckled, looking down at me.

Samuel kneeled; his face close to mine. "You can't really be blaming Hadleigh for all of this, can you? That girl saved your life by not saying anything to her grandfather. Had she told Vittorio about you, there would have been two problems eliminated. Of that, I promise you and Hadleigh wouldn't have been able to stop it," Samuel said, standing up and adjusting his suit jacket. "The fact that she had the bravery to confront me shows just how much she loved you. Stop being foolish."

"Get up and get things ready so you two can get moving," Patch ordered, showing no mercy for my predicament. "And for the love of God, try to remember the girl is carrying your kid and quit upsetting her."

I watched them walk away, so different yet so alike, and scowled as I pushed to my feet. Of course, Samuel was right, just like everyone else that's tried to reason with me. And just when I think I'm on the right track, I just fuck things up again by being a jealous, unreasonable idiot.

"Listen to Samuel," Scotch said, pushing off the side of the building and putting out his cigarette with his boot. "Hadleigh didn't deserve that kind of talk."

"What? Was everyone enjoying the show?" I snapped, still holding my crowning jewels.

"I was already here. You put on the show for free," Scotch stated with a smirk. "Now walk off the knee to the nuts and I'll help you get some shit together. Ava went to talk to Hadleigh and calm her down."

I vowed as I followed Scotch inside to hold my temper from here on out, no matter what. If I had to, I'd walk away and cool off. I shook my head, wondering when the hell I had become such a fucking hothead—the answer—when I fell in love with Haddie.

21

Hadleigh

"I'm sorry, Haddie." Kaven's words felt hollow as I climbed behind him, gripping tightly as we roared down the road. His apology wasn't enough. It was never enough. This constant hurt, the endless accusations—it all cut deep, festering inside me like an open wound.

The ride seemed endless, each mile dragging us further from the clubhouse and deeper into uncertainty. His bike turned onto an old dirt road that was riddled with potholes. Every jolt sent a wave of nausea through me. When a small cabin finally came into view, my stomach clenched tighter. This was the place where he brought Aislynn, not someone *special* like me, but someone he loved.

He killed the motor, and I jumped off, stretching to shake off the fatigue. We should have stopped, but Patch insisted we come directly here, avoiding any chance of being seen.

"You okay?" Kaven asked, his concern clear in his eyes. "You look a little pale."

I took a deep breath, trying to steady myself with the fresh mountain air. "The curves and bumps made me a little nauseous."

"I have some ginger tea inside. It'll help," he said, reaching for my hand. I moved it behind my back and started toward the small porch, not ready for his touch.

With a heavy sigh, he followed, pulling a key from his pocket. "It isn't much, but you should be comfortable enough."

The door swung open, and I marched in, scanning the small space like a soldier on alert. The cabin was unexpectedly warm and inviting. Despite its size, it was cozy, a hidden gem in the secluded forest. It should have been a sanctuary, but it felt like a trap.

I hated it.

I loved it.

I hated that I loved it.

Cheer up, Hadleigh, I scolded myself. Think of all the plants you'll see and the exploring you'll do out here. Kaven moved to the small kitchen area. "I'll make you some tea and while you relax, I'll unload the supplies," he said, setting a kettle on the stove.

"I can do it," I offered, following him.

"Sit down, Haddie," he ordered, pulling down a box from the cabinet. "Let me do this for you."

Lacking the energy to argue, I asked, "Where's the bathroom?"

"Through that door. It's small, but it does the job," he said, relieved that I wasn't going to fight him over a cup of tea.

The bathroom was tiny, no bigger than a closet, but I was grateful for it. Being so far out, such amenities weren't always guaranteed. When I emerged, Kaven was just finishing my tea. "How do you know about what tea can do?"

He placed the mug on the table, and I sat down, taking a sip. "I was taught tea can cure most ailments."

"Your mom taught you, I gather. The first thing she did yesterday was give me a cup," I said with a smile, recalling the memory.

"You got it," he chuckled, touching a strand of my hair and tugging. "I'll unload the supplies, and if you're up to it, we can explore."

"Yeah, you know I won't pass that up," I laughed despite myself. The chance to roam the woods? I wasn't saying no to that. The smells, the sounds, the peace it brought were something I desperately needed.

"That was my hope," he murmured as he headed outside.

I stood, picking up the cup of tea and moving to the small window, gazing at the beauty it revealed. This place was amazing. Already, I felt calmer. In this more relaxed state, I hoped Kaven and I could finally talk without fighting. We were still having a baby together and needed to come to some sort of arrangement.

The sound of the door opening broke my reverie. Kaven walked in, carrying a box of supplies. His movements were careful, almost reverent, as if he feared breaking the fragile peace between us.

"All set," he said, setting the last box down. "Ready to explore?"

I nodded, placing the cup on the windowsill. "Lead the way."

We stepped out into the crisp air, the forest alive with the sounds of nature. Birds chirped, leaves rustled, and somewhere in the distance, a stream murmured softly. Kaven took my hand, and this time, I didn't pull away because, like him, I didn't want to break the tranquility of the moment.

"I want to show you something, and I know you'll love it."

We walked in silence, the tension between us easing with each step. Eventually, we reached a clearing where a beautiful waterfall cascaded, bathed in dappled sunlight. It was breathtakingly beautiful, a hidden paradise.

"I'm ready to go back," I said, starting to turn on my heel, only to have him stop me with a hand on my arm.

"Haddie, I thought you'd love it," he said, looking at me with confusion. "I don't understand you!"

"I do love it!" I cried, tears streaming down my face, hot and bitter.

"Then what's the problem?"

"I'm not the first woman you've brought here to this magical place!" I shouted, watching his eyes widen at my outburst. "It hurts that you have memories of this place with the woman you truly love, the one you brought here to share this place before me. A woman you brought here not because you had to like you did me, but because you wanted to, and it hurts me so much to know that!"

Kaven's face fell, his confusion clear. "Haddie, I—"

"No, you don't get to explain," I interrupted, my voice breaking. "This place, this beautiful place, is tainted for me because I can't stop thinking about her. About how she stood here with you, probably in your arms, probably thinking she was the luckiest woman in the world. And I hate that I'm jealous of her. I hate I feel like I'm competing with another woman in a competition I didn't know I entered."

He reached his hand out, but I stepped back. "I can't compete with your memories, Kaven. I can't keep pretending that this doesn't hurt. It's killing me inside and I would rather be alone for the rest of my life than be someone's second choice!"

His eyes were filled with regret, his voice barely a whisper. "Haddie, I never wanted to hurt you. I brought you here because this place is special to me, and I wanted to share it with you—"

"But you can't erase the memories of her," I interrupted, my voice cracking. "And I can't pretend they don't exist and I'm nothing but a rebound and now an obligation because I got pregnant."

We stood there in the clearing, the sound of the waterfall a cruel reminder of the beauty and pain I was feeling. The paradise Kaven had wanted to show me now felt like a prison, trapping me in the shadows of his past.

I had no idea all the misunderstandings were so deep and affecting her this much. "Haddie, we need to clear all this up right here and right now!" I demanded, desperation lacing my voice as she started to walk away. "Don't walk away and, for once, listen. I don't love Aislynn, and I don't have special memories of her floating around in my head. And I certainly don't see you or our baby as a fucking obligation!"

"Don't play me for a fool, Kaven!" she shouted, her eyes blazing with a mix of pain and fury. "I saw you together, hugging, after you told her you wouldn't change anything that happened!"

She saw me and Aislynn in the hallway. That explained so much. "It's obvious you didn't hear the entire conversation and instead of running, you should have talked to me. That's the first time Aislynn and I had spoken since I've been back. She was just getting closure, nothing more."

"About how much you loved her?"

I looked to the sky in frustration, feeling the weight of my own mistakes. "It's hard to explain, Haddie! I was drawn to Aislynn, and my mind rationalized it as romantic even though inside I knew it wasn't quite right. But what else could it be if not love? I grappled with it for months, leaving for South Carolina to try to sort it out. And then I met you. Suddenly, it was clear what I felt for her wasn't love but wanting to save her, atone for not saving Kezia, just like my brother warned me."

"What are you talking about? Why would you need to save her, and who is Kezia?" she asked, confusion and concern etched across her face.

"Kezia is my sister. She was killed when she was fifteen, and Valley and I were the ones that found her. She was beaten, raped, and left to die in a warehouse near our house. In a lot of ways, I blamed myself. That night Kezia was abducted, she was supposed to be with us, but we blew her off to go to a party at the clubhouse. We thought we were big shit that Valley's dad was letting us crash it for Valley's seventeenth birthday," I explained, my voice breaking.

The pain of speaking about it out loud after so many years was raw, but somehow, with Haddie, it felt less suffocating.

"I'm so sorry, Kaven. It must have been unbearable. But what does that have to do with Aislynn?"

"I can't get into everything. It's her story to tell, but we rescued her from a really bad scene, and every time I saw her, saw the sadness in her eyes, I felt this need to make it go away, to help her heal. When she and Leather fell out, I figured..." I let my words trail off with a heavy sigh. "Haddie, there is no one that comes close to the love I feel for you."

"You love me?" she snapped in disbelief. "What about all those women at the clubhouse? You were with them, I could tell. That's not love."

"I haven't been with anyone since we met. You thought that, and I let you. I'll admit I wasn't a saint before you, but you can't hold me guilty for that," I said, my gaze locking onto hers, pleading. "If it makes you feel better, no other woman has made me only think of her, want only her, and feel this need to be with her all the time. Why would you even think I didn't love you?"

She threw herself into my arms, so relieved I thought she might collapse. "Because, you idiot, you've never said it to me."

"I've said it in my head so many times I guess I thought you knew," I said, my voice softening. The realization that I hadn't told her even once was crazy as hell, since I could have sworn I said it to her every time we had sex.

"What about all the horrible things you've said to me?" she asked, pulling back to look at me, hurt in her eyes.

"I was a stupid ass and you make me fucking crazy, Haddie," I said, pulling her close again. "I get so damn territorial with you and it makes me say and do dumb shit."

"It was really hurtful that you didn't understand how hard things were for me," she whispered against my skin. "Promise me you won't treat me that way again."

"I promise, and something else, when I brought Aislynn to the waterfall, it was to cheer her up and give her some space from Leather. But you, I brought you here thinking it would create the same magic as South Carolina, and I'd get to see you naked under that waterfall looking like the tempting wood fairy I see in my dreams every night."

The intensity of the moment hung in the air, our emotions raw and exposed. I held her tight, hoping she could feel my love through the beat of my heart. She pushed away with a naughty smile on her face. "Let's make the magic happen," she smirked as she removed her clothes slowly in front of me and waded into the water, disappearing with a kick of her feet.

As the sunlight shimmered on the waterfall, I watched as Haddie emerged from the water, every inch of her body glistening with water droplets. My heart pounded in my chest as I took in her naked body, the sight of her making my cock throb painfully in my jeans with the knowledge of what was to come.

I began to undress, unable to take my eyes off her. When I was finally naked, I dove in and swam towards her, my bare feet treading softly on the wet rocks as I stopped in front of her.

Haddie looked at me, her breath catching in her throat as she saw my need for her burning in my eyes. She stepped closer to me, our bodies only inches apart. "Kaven," she whispered, her voice husky with emotion.

Without another word, I pulled her into my arms, my hands cupping her face as I crashed my lips against hers. Our kiss was hungry and demanding, a reflection of the raw attraction that always blazed between us.

My hands roamed over her body, exploring every inch of her skin as our tongues danced wildly together. I nibbled on her ears, causing her to moan softly against my skin. I pulled back slightly, looking into her eyes as I trailed my fingers down her neck and over her collarbone, following the line of her cleavage.

Haddie's breath quickened as she felt my touch, her nipples hardening against my chest. She ran her hands over my back, savoring the feel of my warm skin beneath her fingertips. She traced a line down my spine and over my ass, her fingers leaving a hot trail.

"Do you love me, Haddie?" I asked, my voice rough with the need to be with her.

She nodded her head, her eyes never leaving mine. "More than anything," she whispered.

Without further hesitation, I scooped her up into my arms, carrying her to the nearest flat surface, and I laid her down on the rock, positioning myself between her legs and I ran my hands up her thighs, pushing her legs apart gently.

Haddie gasped as she felt the heat between her legs where my fingers were now expertly teasing her. She arched her back, pressing herself against my touch. "Kaven," she moaned, her hips moving in rhythm with my fingers.

I looked up at her, our eyes locked together as I slowly lowered my head to take one of her nipples into my mouth. She cried out, her back arching even further as I sucked gently on her sensitive nipple.

All the while, my other hand continued to work its magic between her legs, teasing her pussy with a gentle flick of my thumb. I could see her starting to lose control, her breath coming in rapid gasps. She moved her hips in a circular motion against my hand, desperate for release.

I could feel her wetness against my fingers, her body trembling with anticipation. She was so fucking responsive and perfect for me. I moved my free hand down to her heat, opening her up with two fingers, teasing her before I couldn't take it anymore, and thrust my cock inside her. It was so damn hard it was ready to explode, and it was pure torture trying not to cum too fast. She cried out in pleasure, her body arching off of the rock as she met my hard thrusts.

Our movements became more urgent as we neared the end, all too quickly. With one last deep push, I felt myself exploding, unable to hold back any longer, my groans of pleasure mingling with her moans.

Haddie wrapped her arms around me, holding on tight as she felt the heat of our shared experience coursing through her veins. We stayed locked together like that, our hearts pounding in rhythm as we caught our breath.

Finally, we pulled apart, our bodies slick with sweat and dotted with goosebumps. I rested my forehead against hers, our breathing slowing down as we basked in the afterglow of our intense lovemaking.

"I love you, Haddie," I whispered, my voice hoarse from exertion.

She looked into my eyes, seeing nothing but love reflected back at her. "I love you too, Kaven," she replied, her voice equally husky.

22

Hadleigh

"I'm so glad you can cook," I chuckled, watching Kaven move around the small kitchen, effortlessly preparing our dinner. The aroma of sautéed garlic and herbs filled the air, making my stomach growl in anticipation. "I don't know a pot from a pan."

"Don't worry, mama will make it her mission to teach you," he replied with a laugh, his eyes sparkling with amusement. "She fully believes love starts with a full stomach."

I leaned against the counter, mesmerized by his easy movements. "Can I ask what happened to your father?"

Kaven's expression softened as he turned his attention to the sizzling pan. "He died when I was five," he said quietly. "I don't remember much about him except what mama and papu would tell me."

"Papu?" I asked, intrigued.

"Grandfather," he explained, a fond smile touching his lips. "I was his little sidekick, always following him around. He used to bring me up here to this cabin all the time. We'd fish in the lake, hike the trails, and he'd tell me stories about the old days. When he died, he left it to me and it's filled with memories."

"It's beautiful up here," I said, gazing out the window at the serene landscape. The sun was setting, casting a golden glow over the trees. "I could stay in this setting forever and just forget the world."

"Really? You wouldn't miss all the glitz from your rich world?" Kaven asked, a hint of skepticism in his voice.

"I've never needed any of that," I confessed, my voice tinged with bitterness. "I lived like a prisoner. My grandfather had men following me all the time, afraid I would be abducted and used against him. That's how I came to love plants and decided to go into botany. I was never allowed to have a normal childhood, so I spent all my time in the garden with the gardener, learning about plants. It became my peace. That's why I would sneak out at night, because it was the only freedom I had."

Kaven looked at me with understanding in his eyes. "Things aren't going to be easy, Haddie," he said, placing our plates on the table and indicating we sit. The meal he'd prepared was simple but hearty, a testament to his skills in the kitchen. "Your grandfather won't accept me; Samuel made that clear. He's going to fight us getting married, and I don't know what to expect. But I won't back down."

I took his hand in mine, feeling the strength of his resolve and drawing comfort from it. "Neither will I," I promised, squeezing his hand.

"Our lives will be simple. I mean shit, I thought it would be years before I settled down and I'm not really prepared and then there's the club. I can't give that up since it's part of me."

"We'll figure it out," I promised, kissing his cheek. "As long as we're together, I don't care."

"Eat, Haddie," he urged, tapping my plate gently. "I know you didn't eat much today, and we both have to remember the baby. As soon as we get the all-clear, we need to see a doctor."

We began eating, the warmth of the meal and our conversation wrapping around us like a comforting blanket. Kaven talked about the trails he'd explored and the animals he'd seen, his stories painting vivid pictures of the wilderness. I loved the way he described a family of deer he'd encountered on his last visit up here, the grace of their movements, and the way the fawns played without a care in the world, not realizing he watched from the shadows. Kaven was a master storyteller, and I'm guessing he got that from his grandfather.

As we talked, I felt a sense of peace settling over me, a big difference from the constant anxiety of my previous life. "This place feels like a different world," I said softly. "A world where we can just be ourselves."

Kaven nodded, his gaze steady on mine. "It is a different world. Up here, it's just us and nature. No pretense, no expectations. Just life as it should be."

I wished with all my heart we could stay at this cabin forever, shutting out the rest of the world. The reality of our situation loomed over us, but for now, in this moment, we were free. The dying sunlight cast a warm glow on Kaven's face, highlighting the determination in his eyes. We talked during the night between bouts of amazing sex, sharing dreams and fears, our bond growing stronger with each passing moment.

The night was quiet, and the only sounds were the wind blowing through the trees and the occasional call of an owl. As I lay in Kaven's arms, I felt a sense of hope. No matter what challenges awaited us, I knew we would face them together. The cabin, with its memories and promise of new beginnings, had become our special place, and I never wanted it to end.

23

The first light of dawn seeped through the cabin windows, casting a gentle glow over Haddie's sleeping face. I lay there for a moment, watching her breathe, feeling a surge of protectiveness and love. She stirred slightly, murmuring in her sleep, and I smiled, feeling satisfaction at having worn her out. It surprised me that this old bed didn't break with the action it saw last night. My cock twitched at the memory, ready for another go, but I shoved it down. She needed sleep.

I wanted to give her a perfect day, starting with a hearty breakfast and then an activity that I was pretty sure she had never done.

Quietly, I slipped out of bed and headed to the kitchen. I rummaged through the cabinets, finding the ingredients for pancakes. As I mixed the batter, the smell of fresh coffee began to fill the cabin. I knew Haddie would appreciate that because she liked her coffee.

"Haddie," I called softly, peeking into the bedroom. "Wake up, beautiful. It's time for breakfast."

She groaned, pulling the blanket over her head. "Just five more minutes," she mumbled.

"Nope," I said, walking over and gently tugging the blanket away. "No more five minutes. Breakfast is almost ready, and I've got plans for us today."

She opened one eye, giving me a mock glare. "You're too cheerful for this early in the morning."

"Get used to it, with a baby coming we won't see much sleep," I teased, pulling her up and throwing my t-shirt at her to put on. "Come on, I've got coffee waiting."

We made our way to the kitchen, where the table was set with steaming pancakes, fresh fruit, and two mugs of coffee. Haddie's eyes widened in surprise. "Wow, this looks amazing, Kaven."

"Wait until you taste it," I said, handing her a plate. "I might not be a gourmet chef, but I make a mean pancake."

She took a bite, her eyes lighting up. "Okay, you win. These are delicious."

We ate together, laughing and talking about the day ahead. After breakfast, we showered and dressed and then I led her outside, where two fishing poles were propped against the cabin wall.

"Fishing?" she asked, raising an eyebrow.

"Fishing," I confirmed, grinning. "It's a beautiful morning, and there's nothing like catching your own lunch."

She looked at the poles skeptically. "I've never been fishing before. I'm more likely to catch myself than a fish."

"Don't worry, I'll show you," I said, taking her hand and leading her to the small lake. The water was calm, reflecting the clear blue sky above. It was the perfect day for fishing.

We found a good spot on the shore, and I showed her how to bait the hook and cast the line. She watched intently, biting her lip in concentration. When it was her turn, she mimicked my movements, her cast a bit wobbly but successful.

"There you go!" I cheered. "Now we wait."

We sat side by side, our lines bobbing in the water. It was peaceful, and the only sounds were the birds singing and the gentle lapping of the lake. After a few minutes, Haddie's line jerked.

"I think I've got something!" she exclaimed, excitement lighting up her face.

"Reel it in slowly," I instructed, moving closer to help. Together, we pulled in her catch—a small but lively trout.

She laughed, holding the fish up triumphantly. "Look at that! My first fish!"

"Congratulations," I said, laughing with her. "You're a natural."

We continued fishing, and I caught a big one that swayed on the line as I reeled it to shore, water splashing everywhere.

"Hey!" she protested, wiping her face. "Watch where you're aiming that fish juice!"

"Oops," I said, laughing, mesmerized by how pretty she looked bathed in the sunlight, her face lit up with laughter. And I couldn't help but feel grateful. Grateful for the cabin, for the peace it brought, and most of all, for Haddie. She had brought a new kind of light into my life, and I was determined to protect it. For the first time since my sister died, I felt whole, and I wasn't about to blow it.

And just as I had that thought, I saw movement in the tree line across the water. This area was remote and not well known. No one should be up here, but once in a while, an occasional hunter or hiker wandered this way. I hoped that was the case now. "Let's head back to the cabin," I said, pulling Haddie to her feet.

"What's wrong?" she asked, taking my hand as we moved back toward the cabin, my hand ready to grab the pistol I had tucked in the back of my jeans.

"It might be nothing, but I don't want to chance it," I said, stopping when I heard a noise from the brush to my left. "Don't move," I cautioned as I crept into the trees off the side of the path, gun in hand, my eyes darting around the area.

"Kaven!" Haddie shouted and before I could turn around, my world went dark as my body crumpled to the ground.

Hadleigh

My heart pounded as I watched the brutal attack unfold. A hooded figure emerged from behind a tree, smashing something hard against Kaven's head. He crumpled to the ground, unconscious, and a sickening crack echoed through the air. Adrenaline surged through me as I sprinted toward him, heedless of the danger the figure posed.

"Stop, Hadleigh," a cold voice commanded, freezing me in my tracks. My breath caught in my throat as the hooded figure turned toward me, pointing a gun directly at me while lowering the hood with the other hand. Sunlight glinted off the barrel, adding a chilling menace to the scene.

"You...you're the woman from the clubhouse," I stammered, disbelief choking my words. My mind raced to connect the dots. "Why would you do this to him?"

She let out a chilling laugh, the sound echoing ominously through the trees. "It's nothing personal, I assure you. I don't even know him. It's you I want, Hadleigh." A shiver ran down my spine as she mentioned knowing me. "But I must say, you have good taste in men."

"Me? What could you possibly want with me? I don't know you," I replied, my voice trembling. My eyes darted around, seeking an escape or a way to disarm her, but the gun never wavered.

"You'll find out soon enough," she said with a smirk. "But for now, you need to come with me." She stepped closer, her grip tightening painfully on my arm.

I shook her off and tried to run to Kaven again, but she stopped me with a sinister warning. "I'm trying to be nice, Hadleigh. But if you don't do as I say, I'll kill him. You don't want that, do you?"

Tears welled up in my eyes as she pointed the gun at Kaven's motionless body. I had no choice but to comply. Odds were she was after the reward my grandfather offered and wouldn't hurt me. I couldn't risk him being killed; we'd find our way back to each other.

She forced me down a dirt road where a black Jeep awaited us, its windows reflecting the sunlight. The day had become eerily silent, the only sounds the crunch of leaves underfoot and my own ragged breathing. She shoved me into the passenger seat, the leather cold against my skin, and sped off down the mountain road.

"What is this about? The reward?" I demanded, desperation lacing my voice as I clutched the seatbelt, the scenery blurring past.

"Everything will become clear soon," she replied cryptically, swerving to avoid a truck on the narrow road. Her knuckles whitened on the steering wheel. "Just sit still, shut up, and let me drive. These fucking mountain roads are horrendous."

My mind raced with fear and confusion as we descended into the valley, leaving the familiarity of the mountains behind. The silence between us was heavy, punctuated only by the occasional curse as she navigated the winding roads and then onto the interstate. Hours passed, the tension mounting with every mile closer to Philadelphia.

Just outside the city limits, the vehicle took an exit and hit a secondary road. It wasn't long before she turned into a narrow dirt driveway, the Jeep's headlights illuminating the path through a tunnel of trees. We pulled up in front of an old, dilapidated house, its windows dark and foreboding.

The air was thick with the scent of decay and damp earth. She dragged me inside and up the creaking stairs, the wood groaning under our weight. The hallway was lit only by a dirty overhead light, shadows dancing across peeling wallpaper. She unlocked a door at the end and shoved me inside with a force that sent me stumbling. "You have a new roommate," she laughed, the sound hollow and menacing, before slamming the door shut and locking it with a resounding click.

I caught my balance, my eyes adjusting to the dim light from the moon filtering through a small, dirty window. My gaze fell upon a familiar blonde woman sitting on the bed, her eyes widening in surprise. It was the woman living with Samuel in his penthouse. She looked disheveled, her clothes rumpled, and hair tangled.

"Hope?" I whispered, fear gripping me as I realized the full extent of the danger I was in—this wasn't about the reward.

24

THE DEVIL'S HOUSE
West Virginia
Midnight

I groaned as I turned over, pain shooting through my skull like a lightning bolt. My brain scrambled to attention, and then realization dawned. "Haddie?" I called, jerking upright, shaking my head to clear my blurry vision. Panic clawed at my chest as I scanned the surroundings, desperately looking for her.

Fuck, whoever hit me must have taken her. The thought sent a fresh wave of terror through me, and I grabbed the tree for balance as I stood, my legs trembling. The forest spun wildly, and dizziness threatened to send me back to the ground. Fighting the nausea and disorientation, I forced myself to move, each step a monumental effort. I had to get back to the cabin, swaying on my feet as I trudged through the underbrush.

"Kaven?" Fenix's voice cut through the fog in my mind. He emerged from the porch, his face a blurry mask of concern, hurrying toward me. "What happened?"

"They have her," I gasped, barely able to form the words. My legs wobbled as I tried to make my way to my bike, but the world tilted dangerously.

"Hadleigh? Who has her?" Fenix demanded, grabbing me by the midsection and holding me up as I swayed. His grip was the only thing keeping me from collapsing.

"I have to find her," I insisted, my voice raw with desperation. I tried to shake him off, but my strength was failing me.

"Stop it, Kaven," he ordered, his tone firm but laced with worry. "You were hit over the head, you're bleeding. There's no way you can drive in this condition. Get in my truck and I'll take you back to the clubhouse."

I knew he was right, but the urgency to find Haddie was overwhelming. With a frustrated growl, I relented, allowing him to lead me to his truck. He helped me inside, and I slumped against the seat, my head pounding. As we started down the mountain, the gravity of the situation bore down on me like a weight.

"What's going on, Kaven? The truth, and don't give me that bullshit about club business," Fenix demanded, his eyes flicking between me and the road, his knuckles tight on the steering wheel.

Leaning my head back, I exhaled sharply. "It's complicated. Long story short, I was hiding Haddie up here, thinking she would be safe. But that didn't fucking happen!" My voice cracked with frustration and guilt.

"Shit, Kaven, a black Jeep Cherokee almost hit me head-on coming off the access road," Fenix said, slamming his fist on the steering wheel in frustration. "There was some brunette chick driving and a passenger, but I was only focused on the driver."

"Let me have your phone," I demanded, my hands shaking as he handed it over. We were finally in an area with cell service. I quickly dialed the clubhouse, my heart racing. Adam picked up on the second ring.

"I need to talk to Patch now," I barked, feeling the confines of the truck as I waited, every second feeling like an eternity.

"Yeah, talk," Patch growled into the phone. I explained what happened, my words tumbling out in a frantic rush. The details about the black Jeep were crucial. I knew he would get Scotch and Kickstand on it right away. There was no time to waste. "Get your ass back here ASAP," Patch ordered and hung up, leaving a cold dread settling in my stomach.

Fenix glanced at me, worry written all over his face. "You think whoever has Hadleigh will hurt her?"

I sighed, the weight of my failure pressing down on me like a physical burden. "I'm praying this is only about the reward her grandfather is offering. One condition is she has to be returned unharmed." The thought of anything happening to Haddie was unbearable and I should have protected her better. But somehow, someone had found a way to her. It still baffled me how they located the cabin. "What made you come up the mountain?"

"I went to the clubhouse to talk to you since you weren't answering your phone. Of course, they didn't know where you were," he griped, his frustration clear. "So, I figured you had come up to the cabin and decided to check to make sure things were okay. Thank God I did."

I kept my eyes closed, trying to steady my racing heart as the truck sped down the highway. The roar of the engine was a constant reminder of the urgency. Every minute felt like an hour, the distance stretching unbearably between me and Haddie. The thought of her in danger was like a knife twisting in my gut.

Fenix's truck tires hummed against the asphalt, the landscape blurring by as we barreled toward the clubhouse. My mind raced with scenarios, each one worse than the last. I clenched my fists, nails digging into my palms, as if the pain could anchor me in the present and prevent me from spiraling into panic.

"She's strong, Kaven," Fenix said, breaking the tense silence. "Hadleigh's tougher than she looks. She'll hold on until we get to her."

I nodded, though the fear continued to eat at me. Fenix's words were meant to reassure, but the thought of Haddie facing this alone made my chest tighten. "We'll find her," I muttered, more to convince myself than anything.

Minutes ticked by, each one an agonizing wait. The headlights of passing cars seemed to mock our urgency, their bright beams indifferent to our plight. The closer we got to the clubhouse, the more the dread morphed into a burning determination. Whoever took Haddie would regret ever fucking laying a hand on her.

As the clubhouse came into view, a surge of adrenaline coursed through me. We would find her, and I would make sure she never had to fear anything ever again.

25

Hadleigh

"Yes," Hope said, scrambling off the bed. "And you're Hadleigh?"

"The one and only," I replied, scanning the dismal room. "Who is that woman, and what does she want with us?"

"I don't know her name, but from the rough handling and the awful things she's said to me, I think she's a former mistress of Samuel's."

I took a closer look at Hope when she mentioned rough handling and gasped. Bruises mottled her arms, and a fresh handprint stood out on her face. "Are you okay?" My voice trembled. Whoever that woman was, she had been far more abusive to Hope than to me.

"I think so. She only hit me once, muttering about how her partner would kill her if I was hurt." Hope's hand instinctively covered her stomach, and I suspected she was in the same situation as me and I had to know.

"Are you pregnant?"

"Yes," she whispered, her voice breaking. "And I'm terrified of what's going to happen."

"I'm pregnant too," I admitted softly, the reason for Samuel's plan falling into place. He was going to be a father, and I knew he loved Hope.

Her face crumpled, and her eyes locked onto mine. "Is Samuel the father? He promised me..."

"No, Hope," I said firmly. "Samuel and I were never involved. I'm in love with someone else." Relief washed over her features, and I pressed on, "How long have you been here?"

"Since this morning," she replied, sinking back onto the bed. "Samuel must be going crazy trying to find me. I was right behind him, and then everything happened so quickly..."

I sat beside her, squeezing her hand. "He's tearing the city apart, you can count on that. I just hope Kaven is okay. She hit him so hard over the head... the way he crumpled... it was awful."

"Kaven is your boyfriend?"

"Yes, and I'm worried sick about him. That woman is insane," I said, my eyes darting to the door. "We need to get out of here."

"Good luck," she said. "I've searched the room from top to bottom. The only way out is through that window, and it's a death trap."

I hurried to the window, peering down. Long boards with spikes lined the ground below. "It's suicide," I muttered, my heart pounding. "We need another way."

The room fell silent as the lock clicked and the door creaked open. The woman stormed in, gun in hand, and pointed it at Hope. "Come on, my partner is here for you. You're lucky he wants you, or I'd relish making you pay for taking Samuel," she hissed, her eyes wild with fury.

Hope's eyes widened, and she hesitated. "Who is your partner?" she asked, her voice trembling.

"You'll find out," the woman snapped, waving the gun impatiently. "Now move! I want you out of my sight before I put you down like you deserve."

Hope cast a final, desperate glance at me before stepping forward. The door slammed shut and locked behind her. I was left in the stifling silence, more confused and terrified than ever. Why had I been taken? Who was this woman's partner? And why separate Hope from me?

This woman clearly wanted Samuel back and was willing to eliminate anyone in her way. But I couldn't afford to let despair take hold. I had to find a way out and get back to Kaven.

The Devil's House — West Virginia Midnight

"Calm the hell down," Jonesy grumbled, running his fingers over the gash on my head. The sting of antiseptic made me wince. "This cut needs cleaning, and you have a concussion."

"There's no time for this shit," I growled, trying to stand, but Fenix pushed me back down with a firm hand.

"You got time," he said, his voice steady. "They're still tracing that jeep."

"Did you call Bo?" I asked, feeling a fresh wave of pain as Jonesy dabbed at the wound.

"Yeah, him and Cam are heading to the cabin to search the area and bring your bike down the mountain," Fenix replied.

"Church!" Player's voice boomed from across the room. "Now."

"Keep me posted," Fenix said, heading for the door. "I'm going home so Mama doesn't get worried and start asking questions. This would upset her and that's the last thing we want, and Ry is also tracking the Jeep using our resources. We're ready to tear up the highway and have your back." His voice carried a promise of retribution.

Jonesy and I headed down the hallway, my pulse pounding in my ears. Patch and the others were already seated around the table, their faces grim. I grabbed a chair, forcing myself to focus through the haze of pain. "What'd you find out?"

"What I found out is this is a hell of a lot more complicated than we thought," Patch said, his gaze hard.

"Why?" I asked, my stomach knotting.

"Hadleigh wasn't the only one taken today," Patch said, glancing around the room. "Hope, Samuel's woman, is also missing. He's losing his shit, and it turns out she's pregnant, too."

"Again, why?" I pushed, feeling a cold sweat break out on my forehead.

"Still don't know, but it isn't about the reward. This is something else entirely," Patch said, drumming his fingers on the table. The tension in the room was palpable. "We're lucky your brother saw that jeep because it's the only lead we have. Samuel is chomping at the bit to find it and the path it took."

"I can't just sit here and wait," I snapped, the frustration boiling over.

"You won't have to," Patch said. "We're moving out and heading toward Philadelphia to meet Samuel and his men. Whoever took Hadleigh isn't local and will move her to where Hope is. I only need eight men on this because Samuel has an army ready to go. Scotch and Kickstand will relay any information while we're on the move." Patch's gaze locked onto mine. "Hadleigh's grandfather will be informed she was spotted. You can't say anything about her being here. Keep your wits about you, got it?"

"Yeah, I got it," I said, already standing. The thought of Haddie not having to hide anymore fueled my determination. We would find her, and I wouldn't come back without her.

"You ain't riding anywhere," Player snapped, stepping in front of me. "Adam will drive you in the van. You have a concussion, and there's no way you're riding a motorcycle."

"I don't give a fuck as long as we get moving!" I shouted, my voice vibrating off the walls. Patch just shook his head, giving me a pass given the situation with a mumbled, "Watch it, boy."

"Another thing, we are riding no colors, I don't want this club attached to anything. With Amato and his men around, we need to remember the play of just being boot lackeys for Samuel," Patch added, and then signaled we could leave.

I hurried back to my room, shoving what I needed into my backpack before rushing outside. The roar of engines filled the air as the guys prepped their bikes. I jumped into the van, my heart racing. "Let's hit the road," I snapped at Adam, eager to get moving.

26

Hadleigh

The woman strolled back into the room after transferring Hope, her eyes locking onto mine as I stood by the window, lost in thought. She leaned casually against the wall, her gaze piercing and judgmental. "What was Samuel thinking by letting himself get stuck with such an ugly woman?" she sneered, shaking her head in disbelief. "But then I guess that's one of the reasons he wanted to get rid of you."

Her words were meant to cut deep, but I refused to let them hurt me, giving her any satisfaction. "Why am I here?" I demanded, choosing to ignore her venomous insults.

"Because if your grandfather finds you, he'll insist on going through with that silly contract," she explained, her tone dripping with condescension. "And I won't allow that to happen because Samuel belongs to me."

Frustration bubbled up inside me. "Then why not just leave me where I was?" I snapped, turning to face her fully. "And how did you even find me?"

She smirked, twirling a strand of her hair as if this were some trivial game. "I couldn't risk Vittorio finding you," she replied, her eyes studying me intently. "My partner tracked you down at that clubhouse, and I infiltrated it to figure out our next move. It was surprisingly easy, really. Men will do anything for a good fuck. That biker club should work on their security. Anyone could just waltz right in," she chuckled, the sound cold and detached. "But then they moved you after Samuel's visit."

"And yet again, I was safely hidden away. How did you find the cabin?" My voice wavered with a mix of anger and desperation.

She stepped closer, her expression one of smug satisfaction. "My partner searched all the tax records of one Kaven Rafferty—your boyfriend—and found it easily enough. I knew he was the one who had taken you away," she said, her tone growing more predatory as she closed the distance between us. "Now, let's get this finished. I want to be available to console Samuel in the most physical way possible."

Her words sent a shiver down my spine, but I stood my ground, refusing to let her see my fear. The stakes were higher than ever, and I knew I had to find a way to outsmart her, not just for my sake, but for everything I cared about. But as she pointed the gun at me, my heart sank, not having a clue how to make it happen.

THE DEVIL'S HOUSE
West Virginia
Midnight

"**Fuck," I growled as the van jolted when Adam hit** a pothole in the road; the headlights cutting through the darkness. I sat in the passenger seat, my mind racing. The club's bikes roared in front of us, a convoy of determination. My head throbbed with each bump, but I forced myself to focus.

"We're gonna find her, man," Adam said, his voice steady. "We've got eyes everywhere."

I nodded, clenching and unclenching my fists. "We better. Every minute that passes..."

"I know," he interrupted, glancing at me. "We'll get her back." Adam was a childhood friend of mine and Valley, even though he was a few years younger than us and an all-around good guy.

The radio crackled to life, Scotch's voice breaking through. "We've got a lead. The jeep took exit 330 off interstate I-76 and disappeared. They're scouring the back roads now with google maps to see what's around the area."

"Heard that," Adam replied. He pressed down on the accelerator, the van's engine growling in response.

I grabbed the mic and shouted, "Patch, what's the plan?"

"We're splitting up," Patch's voice came through, crackling with static over the sound of his motorcycle. "Half of us will cover the interstate exit left and the other half right, combing the back roads. Samuel's men are already on the ground and heading in the same direction."

"Got it," I said, my heart pounding harder. "We'll follow left."

Minutes felt like hours as we raced down the highway, the tension

Midnight

in the van thickening with each passing mile. I glanced out the window, the landscape a blur of shadows and fleeting lights as we took the exit and our group parted.

"Think they'll try to hole up somewhere off the beaten path?" Adam asked, breaking the silence.

"Depends on who they're working with," I replied, my mind piecing together possibilities. "It's a long shot finding them, but I'm not about to give up."

My eyes scanned the darkness as we slowed down at each driveway and road we saw. Then there it was—a black jeep sitting in front of what looked to be a vacant house, except it wasn't because a light shined inside.

The radio crackled again as I picked it up. "Midnight here. We've got a location on the jeep, five miles left off the exit, parked at an old house. I'll ping the location. Looks like they're trying to lie low, house looks vacant."

"On our way, stay still till we get there," Patch said, as my gut twisting with a mix of hope and fear. "If they move follow, don't let them slip away."

"Understood," came the chorus of replies.

The old house loomed ahead, a dark silhouette against the night sky as the van skidded to a halt a short way down the road, and I jumped out, the night air cool against my fevered skin. The roar of bikes filled the air as the club pulled in behind us.

"Form a perimeter!" Patch barked, dismounting his bike. "Don't let your guard down!"

I scanned the area, eyes narrowing. The jeep was parked haphazardly, its engine still ticking as it cooled. "There!" I pointed, seeing a shadow pass in the low light.

"Move out!" Patch ordered; his voice hushed.

We spread out, moving quickly but cautiously. My heart pounded in my chest, each step bringing me closer to Haddie. I tightened my grip on the pistol at my side, ready for whatever came next.

Samuel and his men joined us, their presence a silent but powerful reinforcement. We surrounded the house, the tension crackling in the air. I approached the front door, my senses on high alert. Nothing but silence reached my ears, and I motioned for the others to follow as we entered through the front door, which wasn't even locked.

We all spread out, searching the place, and a small thud sounded from upstairs, and Samuel and I headed that way, knocking open the doors as we went down the hallway until finally, we got to the last door, which was locked.

Samuel motioned for his man to kick the door open. The old wood splintered under the force, and we stormed inside. The room was dark, shadows from the moon dancing in the corners. "Help." Her faint voice sounded from somewhere close. I moved toward the sound of her voice, my pulse racing.

"Haddie, where are you?" I called, my voice echoing through the empty room.

"In here!" Her voice was stronger now, closer.

"She's under the bed," I shouted, shoving the bed away from the wall.

Sure enough, under the bed was a small door, and we scrambled to open it, finding her tied up and bruised but alive. Her eyes widened with recognition. "Hold on, Haddie," I whispered, rushing to pull her out. "We're getting you out of here."

27

Hadleigh

Relief, unlike anything I'd ever known, shot through me as I locked eyes with Kaven. Moments ago, I was certain I'd die in this decrepit house, my existence erased without a trace. The woman, despite my desperate pleas, refused to listen to reason. Her cold response played in my mind: "You are an inconvenience."

She had tied me up, stuffing me into a cramped hole beneath the bed, and was about to pull the trigger. I had decided then and there to do something, and my feet lifted, ready to knock her off balance, when her phone rang. An urgent conversation followed before she slammed the door shut on me, and I heard her footsteps retreating.

"Kaven," I breathed, my voice trembling.

"Are you hurt?" he asked, his hands frantically checking me over before pulling me close.

"Hope? Where is Hope?" Samuel demanded, his voice laced with panic as he leaned down, his eyes wild with fear.

"They moved her," I said, clinging to Kaven as he helped me up, his arms never leaving me.

"Who are they? Tell me!" Samuel shouted at me, and at that moment, as I looked into his eyes, I realized why our world feared him.

"I don't know," I whispered, my apology clear in my eyes. "The woman mentioned a partner who wanted Hope. She said Hope was lucky because otherwise, she'd have killed her. She was so rough with her, so full of hate."

"We found a woman hiding in the basement," Player announced, entering the room. "We have her cornered."

"That's her," I said, my voice shaky. "Someone tipped her off just before she was about to..." My words faltered as the reality of how close I came to death washed over me.

"Your grandfather is on his way. You don't know who took you or why?" Samuel whispered before hurrying to the basement.

"Are you sure you're not hurt?" Kaven asked, pulling me into a fierce embrace.

"Just bruises and a good scare, but I'll be fine. I just want out of here," I replied, holding onto him just as tightly.

"Come on," he said, guiding me downstairs. As we stepped out the front door, several vehicles screeched to a halt in the driveway. I sighed, recognizing that the fight was far from over as my grandfather and his men jumped out, guns drawn.

"Hadleigh, honey, are you okay?" he asked, pulling me from Kaven, his eyes scanning me with worry that slowly turned to relief. "Who did this?"

"I don't know," I lied, shaking my head. "Masked men took me from the garden, then a woman kept moving me from place to place." A gunshot rang out from inside the house, and I knew Samuel had pulled the trigger, silencing her forever.

Grandfather signaled his men to check inside and took my arm. "Let's get you home."

Kaven stepped forward, his grip firm on my arm. "Haddie is coming with me," he said, his voice steely and eyes hard.

I placed a hand on Kaven's chest and met my grandfather's confused gaze. "I love and want to be with Kaven, and I won't marry anyone but him."

"Haddie?" Vittorio questioned, raising an eyebrow as his eyes scanned over me. Something flickered behind that hard gaze, a shadow of something—recognition? "Take him back to the house," he ordered. Two men converged on me, gripping my arms with bruising force.

"No!" Haddie shouted at Vittorio, her voice breaking through the tense air as she jumped in front of me.

The sound of guns being cocked echoed around us, my club brothers making it clear they wouldn't let this happen without a fight. Vittorio's men countered, the standoff teetering on the edge of violence. I glanced at Patch, who was ready for battle, and said, "It's okay. I want to go and settle everything. It's the only way."

The tension stretched for agonizing moments before Vittorio spoke. "Put your guns down. The boy won't be killed, I promise you. I just have a few questions for him."

Reluctantly, the guns were lowered, and I was led to one vehicle, not the same one as Haddie. Our eyes met, her gaze filled with a determination that mirrored my own before I was pushed inside.

Samuel and his men rushed out of the house in a blur of motion. Without a word, they jumped into their vehicles and peeled out of the driveway. He must have gotten the information he needed before dealing with the woman.

Two men flanked me as the cars sped back onto the interstate. As the city lights came into view, my determination solidified. Vittorio would have to accept this, or his only alternative would be to kill me. I tried not to dwell on that dark possibility because, despite his promise to Patch, it was a genuine worry.

The cars slowed at a massive set of gates that creaked open, revealing a long, winding driveway. We stopped in front of an enormous house—no, a mansion. I was led inside, and my eyes widened at the luxury. The place even smelled rich. For a moment, doubt flickered—could Haddie truly be happy with a man like me, without all this wealth? I shoved the thought aside. Haddie wasn't superficial. We would be fine.

The men took me down a set of stairs and shoved me into a cold concrete room with drains on the floor. A wooden chair sat ominously in the center. "Mr. Amato will deal with you shortly," one of them growled before slamming the door and locking it with a decisive click.

I looked around and laughed bitterly. Of course, a Mafia boss would have a torture cell in his house. The room felt like a tomb and I took a deep breath, pacing back and forth, waiting for Vittorio to arrive so I could have my say.

28

Hadleigh

Grandfather led me into his office, his silence during the ride home a looming storm. "Take a seat, Hadleigh," he instructed, his voice as stern as stone.

I sat down, inhaling deeply to steady my nerves. "It wasn't intentional, us falling in love. It just happened."

He settled behind his desk, leaning forward, his eyes boring into mine. "How did you even meet this man? Why wouldn't I know about this? Does he work for Samuel?" His voice was a low, dangerous whisper.

"It's complicated. We met in South Carolina," I replied, weaving partial truths with caution. I couldn't reveal the intimate details of our relationship. "Mother found out and brought me home. I never thought I'd see him again. It broke me. But then there he was, rescuing me." Lying to my grandfather felt like a betrayal, but I had promised Samuel. Too many lives depended on my silence.

His gaze never wavered, his eyes searching mine for any sign of deceit. "You know I can't allow you to marry this man. Not only do I have a contract with Samuel, but he has nothing to offer you," he said, leaning back. "I won't let my granddaughter marry a nobody."

I leaned forward, meeting his gaze with unwavering determination. "You have no choice. I'm pregnant with his child," I announced, my heart pounding as I watched his face shift from calm to fury.

"You're joking," he snarled, leaping from his chair to loom over me. "How could that be possible if you haven't seen him since South Carolina?"

Summoning all my courage, I stood to face him. "I'm almost four months along." I stretched the truth, remembering Samuel's words. "When I found out, I didn't know what to do. Then I was taken, but now Kaven and I have been reunited. I want to be with him," I said, my voice trembling as tears threatened to fall. "I love him."

"Do you understand the position you've put me in by being so careless?" he scolded, his voice softening slightly. "I can only hope Samuel will understand. I can't expect him to accept a child that's not his, but that doesn't mean I'll let you marry someone outside our circle."

"Then I'll run away," I declared with fierce resolve. "If you try to stop it or hurt Kaven, I will leave and never return." With that, I fled his office, already showing too much weakness. I've learned over the years he could smell it a mile away and pounce.

Grandfather's office door slammed shut behind me, the echo reverberating through the silent house. My heart raced as I fled down the hallway, the weight of his anger pressing down on me. My mind was a whirlwind of fear and determination. I couldn't let him control my fate.

The night air hit me as I stepped outside, cool and refreshing, but it did little to calm the emotion raging inside me. The greenhouse loomed ahead, a sanctuary in the storm of emotions I was feeling. I stumbled inside, my legs barely able to carry me. The sweet, earthy scent of the plants wrapped around me, a glaring difference to the suffocating tension of the house.

I threw myself onto the swing, its creaking the only sound in the stillness. Tears finally spilled over, hot and unrelenting. The swing rocked gently, its motion a feeble attempt to soothe my shattered nerves. I clutched my stomach, whispering promises to my unborn child, swearing to protect them and Kaven at any cost.

The rocking should have put me to sleep, except every creak and rustle outside the greenhouse set my heart racing with fear they would hurt Kaven. My grandfather's threats played in my mind, a constant reminder of the danger that was still possible. But amid the fear, a steely resolve began to harden within me. I would fight for my love, for my child. I would not let Grandfather split us apart.

Suddenly, the door creaked open, the sound like a gunshot in the tense silence. Vittorio stepped in, surprisingly alone, his presence dominating the room. His piercing eyes, the exact shade of Haddie's, locked onto mine with an intensity that made my blood run cold. He knew.

He knew she was pregnant.

"Sit," he commanded, pointing to the chair.

My heart pounded so loudly I was sure he could hear it. This was the moment of truth. My future—and Haddie's—hung in the balance. "I don't want to sit in the chair," I said, my voice steady despite the adrenaline coursing through me. "We can talk just fine standing."

"Fine," he smirked, his eyebrow arching in surprise at my defiance. He looked me over, his gaze a mix of curiosity and contempt. "I've been informed you played where you had no business playing."

"Haddie isn't some playground with a fenced gate that only you can determine who comes into her circle. We met, fell in love, end of story," I said, my voice hardening with each word. "And nothing aside from death will keep her and my baby from me."

"That can be arranged," he snarled, his fists clenching at his sides. The menace in his voice was unmistakable. "You have nothing to offer Hadleigh and her child. You're a biker, a nobody. How will you even provide for them?"

"Just like every normal family in America, I'll work to provide and create a home for them," I shot back, standing my ground. "Money isn't everything."

"Not everything, but it makes life much easier. I don't think Hadleigh understands how hard life will be for her without money."

"I didn't have money growing up, but I had a family that loved me, way better than this museum of a house," I retorted, catching a flicker of something — again was it recognition—in his eyes. Had he already done a background check on me?

"What if I were to pay you to go away?" he asked, his eyes narrowing as he sized me up. "Enough to set you up for life. Let me take care of Hadleigh and the child and release you from the burden."

"Burden?" I spat, my anger boiling over. "Is that how you see them? You mafia assholes are a cold bunch! Take your money and use it to buy something to warm up your cold soul because I don't need it."

He shook his head, muttering something under his breath I couldn't catch. Then, his eyes pinned me again. "How did you come to rescue Hadleigh? Are you doing work for Samuel?" The suspicion in his voice was razor-sharp.

"Samuel and our club president are brothers; we have several hackers in our club who can find out shit on the underground that nobody else can. He hired us to help find his lost fiancée, and that's when I realized Hadleigh was my Haddie and there was no way I wasn't going to be part of it," I explained, praying it all made sense.

"And how did you find out she was pregnant? She confessed she only knew after you were separated."

"I didn't find out until tonight, just like you," I said, my eyes never leaving his. "But even without her telling me she was pregnant, I would still be fighting for us."

He studied me for what felt like an eternity, his eyes cold and calculating. My breath was shallow, each second dragging out painfully. "My men will move you to a room more comfortable until I make my decision. I still have a few things to consider," he finally said, turning on his heel and leaving before I could respond.

His men appeared almost instantly, their grip on my arms firm as they escorted me down a hallway. They shoved me into a bedroom and the door clicking shut behind me with a finality that made my heart sink. "Food has been brought for you," one of them muttered before the lock slid into place.

Dammit, I was locked in, and there was no chance to find and talk to Haddie. I needed to know she was okay and not hurt. Everything happened so fast and sometimes when the adrenaline goes away you notice things. I took a deep breath, pacing the room. The only choice I had was to wait and get ready to fight.

29

I sat behind my desk, tapping my fingers against the wood, my mind racing to process the whirlwind of events from the past few hours. Relief at finding Hadleigh unharmed had quickly turned into shock upon learning she was pregnant. Now, I had no choice but to break the contract with Samuel. I doubted he'd be upset; he and Hadleigh had never truly connected. Still, I had hoped they might grow fond of each other. Samuel's heart, however, was elsewhere, with someone else.

I knew exactly how he felt, having experienced the same situation.

A sharp knock on the door jolted me, signaling my visitor's arrival. The door swung open, and I steeled myself for a confrontation

I never thought I'd face again. "Where is my son?" Mona demanded, storming into my office with a fiery determination that time had not dimmed. Despite the years, she was still as breathtaking as ever.

I stood, concealing the torrent of emotions that surged inside me at the sight of her. "He's being taken care of," I said, clenching my fists to keep from reaching for her.

"I don't believe you. Let me see him," she insisted, her eyes blazing with fury. "You have no right to hold him, Vito."

"On the contrary, I have every right," I countered, leaning on my desk, trying to maintain my composure. "Your son thinks he can take my granddaughter away from me."

"She's pregnant with his child, and he loves her," Mona snapped. "Why stand in their way?"

"Because I can't bear to see her marry someone who's the spitting image of the man who stole you from me, a constant reminder of what I lost!" I roared, slamming my fist on the desk. "I knew he was Cameron's son the moment I saw him."

"What you lost?" she shot back, her voice shaking with emotion. "I wasn't yours to lose, Vito."

"You loved me!" I reminded her, my voice rising in frustration.

"And where did that get me?" she yelled, tears welling in her eyes. "Huh, Vito? You wanted me as a dirty secret. You had a wife and child, remember?" Her voice softened with pain. "You didn't love me like I loved you."

"That's not true, Mona," I hissed. "I would have taken care of you, but you ran off and married Cameron."

"Why wouldn't I marry Cameron? He loved me, was there for me every day while you were off doing business and spending time with your family!" she cried. "We were together because you assigned him to watch me like I was a prisoner."

"I loved you!" I said, pounding my chest. "And the proof is I didn't kill Cameron for what he did! I did that for you because, by the time I found you, he had already gotten you pregnant. Despite my anger, I still watched out for you from afar."

"What do you mean?" she asked, her voice trembling.

"Do you really think your father had the funds to take care of you and your children after Cameron died?"

"He wouldn't have taken money from you."

"But he did. He knew how hard it would be without it," I told her. "I paid for Kezia's funeral," I said softly, knowing how deeply losing her daughter had hurt.

She turned away, trying to hide the impact of my words, then faced me again, her eyes filled with a storm of emotions. "None of that matters now. Too much time has passed, and my only concern is Kaven. I want to see him, Vito."

"Well, Mona, what happens next is up to you," I said, almost reaching for her but pulling back. It was too soon.

"Up to me? How?" she asked, confusion mingling with suspicion.

"If I allow Kaven to marry Hadleigh, there will be conditions," I said, watching her face shift from confusion to curiosity. "The first condition is I want you to have dinner with me at least once a month. Let us reconnect."

"What about..." she began, but I cut her off.

"I've been alone for many years now. My wife and son are gone. I'm free to do as I please, and I want to spend time with you," I said, my gaze lingering on her face.

"Is this some sort of game to punish me for leaving you? I'm not a young woman anymore, and I'm sure with your power and money, you already have someone," she said, sadness creeping into her voice. "You lure me back in only to dump me cruelly?"

"No, Mona, I don't, and I won't. We've both aged, me more than you, but I still see the same beautiful woman who stole my heart," I said, my voice earnest. "Are you afraid of what you still feel? Is that why you never remarried?"

Her eyes revealed the truth. She still had feelings for me and after a moment, she replied, "What are your other conditions?"

"Those are for your son, if you agree to your condition," I said.

"Fine, Vito, I agree, but you have to come to me since this was your idea," she demanded, lifting her chin defiantly, putting her pretty nose in the air like a queen.

"Not a problem," I replied, barely able to contain my relief. "Have a seat while I have a word with Kaven before bringing him to see you."

With a frustrated huff, she sat on the edge of the sofa. "My two boys, Ry and Fenix, are waiting for me. Tell them I'll be right out before they worry."

I nodded, a smile playing on my lips as I left my office to speak with Kaven. The boy was lucky I loved his mother, or he'd be facing a very different fate.

West Virginia Midnight

I jumped from the chair as soon as the door opened, and Vittorio strode in. My patience had run out. "I'm done with this game you're playing, Vittorio," I snarled.

"I don't play games," he replied calmly. "Those are for children."

"Let's settle this now," I demanded, facing him squarely.

"Before I agree to this marriage between you and Hadleigh, I have a few conditions," he said, his tone dripping with authority.

"I don't have to agree to anything you demand," I shot back, glaring at him.

His eyes hardened, and a smirk curled his lips. "Yes, you do, because despite what you think, I can make you disappear."

I knew he could, but I wasn't about to back down. "Just spit out your demands so we can get this over with and I can see Haddie."

"First condition, you and Hadleigh will marry here at my home, giving her the wedding she deserves," he began, pausing for my response.

"I want Hadleigh to have a nice wedding, so fine. I agree."

"Second, I will have access to Hadleigh and my great-grandchild. Third, I will gift you a proper house for them. Fourth, you will get a real job and quit that motorcycle club you're running with. I want you to work for me."

"I can provide everything they need," I snarled. "And I can work and still be a part of my club. I'm not changing who I am for you or anybody. This is all about control for you, but you don't own me and never will."

The door flew open, and Haddie rushed in, Vittorio's men at her heels. "Sorry, boss, she ran in before we could stop her."

"Just close the damn door," Vittorio snapped, his eyes locking on Haddie. "This is between me and Kaven."

"I already heard your conditions," she said with a smirk. "That wall is thin as paper, for future reference," she added, pointing to a side wall.

"Hadleigh, you're overstepping here," he warned.

"We accept the wedding, access to me and my baby, and a house of our choosing in West Virginia," she pressed. "But that's it. Our life is our own, and we will live it that way."

"Hadleigh, don't push your luck with me," he growled. "I don't have to accept anything; I can make what I want happen."

"Like make Kaven disappear?" she challenged, having overheard his earlier threat. "I'll disappear right along with him. There's always a way, and I'll find it. You know I will."

"Alright, let's do this," he relented. "I will accept those conditions, since I will be in the area frequently to see someone. I agree, as long as I see you and the child well cared for, and I don't just mean money." He pointed at me. "He's part of a biker club, Hadleigh. Do you know what goes on at those clubhouses? Do you? Because I can promise you those men aren't faithful."

"Now just a fucking minute!" I snarled, stepping toward him, fists clenched. "You don't know shit."

"I trust him," Haddie said, stepping between us, her hand on my chest. "I know he loves me and won't ever jeopardize that for anything. Plus, the men under you, and including you when grandmother was alive, cheat on their wives all the time. It would have happened in the loveless marriage you were forcing me into. I know all about how marriages work in our circle, grandfather."

Vittorio's eyes softened a bit, and he took a moment before speaking. "You're right, Hadleigh, and I shouldn't have pushed a loveless marriage on you. It's hell when you find your true love." He sighed. "I accept your terms. Come with me. Someone is waiting to see you."

We walked down several long hallways and descended the largest staircase I had ever seen before, stopping in front of a door that was immediately opened by a guard, letting us inside. "Kaven!"

Before I could even process it, Mama hugged me tightly and then stepped back, looking me over. "Mama? What are you doing here?"

30

"I'll explain everything later," Mama whispered, pulling me into another tight hug, relief in her voice. "I just need to reassure myself that you're okay."

I gently moved her aside, fury boiling in my veins, and turned on Vittorio with a snarl. "Did you threaten her? Bring her here to intimidate me? Use her as some kind of pawn?"

"Don't test my patience," he growled, his eyes flashing with anger. "You're getting more than I ever intended. You're too much like your father for my liking, so tread lightly."

"My father? What do you know about my daddy?" I spat, every word dripping with suspicion.

"Enough, Kaven," Mama interjected sharply, stepping between us. "I said I would explain later when all my sons are together." She turned to Haddie, pulling her into a tight embrace. "I'm happy you're safe. I worried for you and the baby."

"We're both okay," Haddie assured her, though her voice wavered slightly.

Vittorio cleared his throat. "I've called a doctor who will be here shortly to check you over. Being this far along without medical care is reckless."

"It's not like I had a choice," Haddie retorted, just as the door burst open. A woman dressed to the nines stormed in, her eyes wild and frantic as they locked onto Haddie.

"Hadleigh!" she cried, rushing forward to envelop Haddie in her arms. She pulled back, scanning her daughter's face with a desperate intensity. "Thank God you're safe. They told me you were unharmed."

"Yes, Mother, I'm fine. It was terrifying, but I'm okay," Haddie replied, glancing nervously at Vittorio.

Her mother's gaze swept the room, landing on me and Mama with thinly veiled disdain. "What's going on here? Who are these people?"

"This is Kaven and his mother," Haddie said, moving to stand beside me, her hand gripping mine tightly. "Kaven is the man from South Carolina."

Her eyes widened in shock, then narrowed in suspicion. "Why are they here?"

"Because Jenny, Hadleigh is almost four months pregnant," Vittorio snapped, his tone cold and accusatory. "Apparently, you didn't step in soon enough."

Jenny's face blanched, her eyes snapping back to Haddie in horror. "Hadleigh, how could you be so careless?" Her gaze turned icy as it moved over me and Mama. "This is unacceptable."

Haddie's eyes flashed with defiance. "Let's talk about this in private," she said, taking her mother by the arm and leading her to the door. "Now."

The door clicked shut behind them, leaving a suffocating silence in their wake. I turned to Mama, my mind racing with unanswered questions. "I want to know what you being here is about."

Before she could respond, Vittorio's phone buzzed. He glanced at the screen, his expression darkening. "I was informed all of your sons have arrived and are ready to start a war. If you'll follow me, I'll take you to them, and you can explain everything, Mona," he said, opening the door and signaling us through. As they exchanged a knowing look, I noticed a softness in Vittorio's eyes when he looked at her—a softness I hadn't seen from him before.

"Mona?" I questioned, my eyebrows shooting up. "Why are you calling my mama by her given name?"

"I'll explain, Kaven. Now hush and come on," Mama scolded, her voice stern but trembling slightly. The tension was palpable as I followed them down the hall, my mind churning with confusion about how they knew each other.

"Mama," my brothers shouted as we walked into the room, Vittorio closing the door behind us. The air was thick with unspoken tension. "What's going on here?" Ry demanded, his voice edged with suspicion.

Mama sighed heavily, the weight of her words pulling at her shoulders. "Sit and listen."

We all sat, the room buzzing with curiosity and apprehension. She began, "When I was nineteen, I came to this city with my friend Rosa to work at a high-end restaurant. There was no work in our town and times were hard. While I was there, I met Vito Amato. He would come in often, and before long, we were in a relationship."

"What are you saying?" Cam interrupted, disbelief stark in his voice. "Surely you didn't fall for a man in the mafia?"

"Don't interrupt me," she snapped, her eyes flashing. "In those days, we didn't have the internet to google everything. I had no idea he was in the mafia. I thought he was a well-off businessman." She looked away, her gaze distant and haunted. "Before long, he confessed his love, and moved me into his apartment. I thought I was on top of the world."

She paused, her face contorted with pain. "Until one day, I was out running errands and ran smack into Vito... and his wife and child." A single tear slipped down her cheek, the room heavy with silence. "I had no idea he was married. I remember running back to the apartment, gathering my things to leave. But I never made it out the door. Vito had sent his men to make sure I couldn't leave."

"He held you prisoner?" Ry growled, his fists clenching, eyes blazing with fury.

Mama took a deep breath, her voice trembling. "Yes, though Vito saw it differently. He thought I'd get over it and accept being the other woman. Vito wasn't willing to let me go, so he assigned a guard to me named Cameron."

"Daddy?" I asked, my voice barely a whisper, heart pounding in my chest.

"Yes," she nodded. "Vito left on an overseas trip for a few months. Cameron and I spent all our time together. We were both Roma, shared the same background. Vito thought that would comfort me. It did, but not how he imagined. Cameron and I fell in love, and he convinced me to run away with him. I didn't hesitate, even though I knew it was dangerous. The rest, you already know—we came back to my hometown, got married, and had all of you."

"And Vito didn't retaliate?" Fenix asked, eyes wide with shock. "That doesn't sound right."

"He knew where we went," she said, a bittersweet smile forming. "But since I was pregnant and married, he let it go because he loved me."

"I'm not..." Ry stammered, horror dawning on his face, the weight of his question heavy in the air since he was the oldest.

Mama reached over and smacked him lightly across the head. "Of course not! You all belong to Cameron!"

"So, what does he want from you?" I asked, fearing what he was making her do. "I know he demanded something to let me have Haddie."

"One dinner a month to get to know each other again," she replied, her voice barely audible.

"No fucking way," we all shouted, standing up in unison, outrage coursing through us. "You know he's a criminal—the damn mafia!" Grey spat, his eyes blazing.

"Don't you dare talk to your mama like that," she shouted back, standing tall, eyes fiery. "You think I'm blind? I can take care of myself. It's one dinner a month, not marriage. Watch yourselves, because no matter how old you get, I can still take a switch to you."

"You don't have to do this," I said, grabbing her hand, my voice urgent, desperate.

"No, I do," she replied, smiling sadly, determination in her eyes. "Vito is strong-willed and overbearing. He will interfere with what you and Hadleigh try to build. But with me helping control Vito, things will go smoother for you two. I want to see you happy."

I hugged her tightly, gratitude and love swelling in my chest. "Let's find Haddie and get out of here," I whispered. I feared Vittorio would change his mind, and I wanted us far away from this place.

Hadleigh

"Hadleigh, how could you do this?" My mother's voice sliced through the silence like a knife as I closed the door behind me. I walked to the window, staring out at the sprawling estate, trying to steady my racing heart. The weight of the conversation ahead bore down on me.

"It happened, and nothing can change it," I said, turning to face her. "We are getting married, and I'm moving to West Virginia."

"I don't think so, young lady!" she snapped, her eyes blazing with a fury I hadn't seen in years. "Your grandfather will take care of this. There won't be a wedding to that man."

"He's already agreed," I replied, watching her expression shift from fury to disbelief. The color drained from her face. "We've already negotiated the terms."

"You're lying!" she spat, her voice trembling. "Vittorio would never agree to let you marry outside of our inner circle, and his contract with Samuel Flavio is still intact."

"Mother, listen to me," I said, struggling to keep my voice calm despite the storm brewing inside me. "Kaven and I are getting married, and nothing will change that. Grandfather has agreed, so stop being difficult. His family are good people."

"Why do you have to move? You and your baby should be here, with us," she said, her tone softening with a hint of sadness. The sight of her breaking heart pierced through my resolve. I was her only child, and I was leaving.

"Mother, it's not that far away. We'll still see each other regularly, but if I stay here, grandfather will try to control every move we make, and I refuse to live like that."

She sank slowly onto the sofa, her tear-filled eyes searching mine. "You're right, but I hate the thought of you leaving. I always thought you'd be close enough to see every day. I'm surprised Vittorio agreed."

I laughed, feeling relief at her acceptance. "One condition was that he has access to me and my child, so he plans on being around quite a bit."

She smiled, her eyes brightening despite the tears. "And I will be too. A grandchild... I can't wait."

"Just don't be rude to Kaven and his mother," I warned, feeling the protective edge in my voice. "They don't deserve it. Money doesn't make the person, and you should know that by now."

"Fine, but my grandchild will still have the best of everything. On that, I won't back down," she insisted, standing and straightening her dress with an air of finality. "Now, I suppose I should go meet this Kaven and his mother."

As we walked down the hall, my mind raced with a hundred

thoughts and fears. One thing was for sure: life with Kaven and our families would never be dull. They were going to keep us on our toes, and I could only hope we were ready for the challenge.

31

The Devil's House
West Virginia
Midnight

"Jesus Haddie," I groaned as she twisted her hips as she rode me. "I won't last long if you keep doing that."

Her hands ran over my chest as she leaned down to kiss me and breathed, "Just enjoy the ride."

"That's easier said than done," I muttered against her lips, stealing another sweet taste of her.

Laughing softly, she traced a finger down my cheek and moved her hips in that slow, sensual rhythm again. The sight of her, the feel of her, it was so fucking good. Her long hair was cascading down around us, creating an intimate curtain that shut out the rest of the world. It was just Haddie and me.

She straightened back up and ran her hands up my torso, clutching at my shoulders. The sudden shift had me gasping, my hands automatically gripping her hips to guide her. Her head tilted back, and she let out a low moan. The sound echoed through the small cabin, imprinting itself into the walls.

"I can't stop..." I began, trying to offer what little control I had left.

"And here I thought you were a tough guy," she teased lightly. The smile on her face was wickedly hot, a sight for the thirsty man lost in the desert for months. It was a challenge, one I willingly accepted.

"Oh Haddie," I smirked defiantly, flipping us over so she was under me now. "I'm tougher than you think."

Her surprise quickly turned into a delighted squeal before morphing into soft moans as I claimed her lips with mine once more, taking over. The tables had been turned, and it was time for her to 'enjoy the ride'.

Her hands moved to my hair, strands of it weaving through her fingers as she arched upwards, meeting me halfway. My lips tasted the sweet saltiness of her skin as I traced a path downwards from her lips along the curve of her neck. She gasped, her nails digging into my scalp, sending jolts of pleasure mixed with pain coursing through me.

She writhed beneath me, pure unfiltered passion emanating from every move she made, every soft whimper escaping her lips. I marveled at the sight of her, so fucking turned on by the fact she was mine.

With a growl of pure need, I began moving against her, setting my own pace that was both punishing and loving. Her body moved perfectly in sync with mine, a testament to our special connection. There was no more talking, only the sound of shared breaths and quiet sighs of pleasure filled the room.

"Oh God," she gasped as I drove into her deeper, harder. Her fingers dug into my back; her legs wrapped around my waist, bringing me closer. The friction between us created an inferno that consumed all rational thought.

As I watched Haddie's face, a new wave of urgency swept over me. Without uttering a single word, our bodies spoke volumes. Our bodies began to move faster, the bed bouncing off the floor. Her fingers traced hot trails over my back, pressing into me with a feral need that matched my own. Fucking hell, there's nothing like the pleasure she gives me.

Her breath hitched as I reached between us, eliciting a high cry as my hand found her most sensitive spot. "God," she swore, the low moan rumbling through her chest and vibrating against my own. I could feel her body tightening around me, ready to tip over the edge.

She tugged at my hair, pulling me up to meet her gaze. Our eyes locked and in their fiery depths, I saw everything - the lust, need, love - all mirrored in my own irises. I felt like I was drowning in them, but it was a blissful descent that I didn't mind in the least.

Her moans grew louder and more desperate, the sweetest music to my ears, her body arching as the pleasure mounted. The moment was near, I could sense it in the frantic pace of her breathing and in the increasingly tight coil of her body.

"Don't stop," she rasped out, her voice barely a whisper among our labored breathing and pounding hearts. "Please..."

The plea was my undoing. My control shattered like a thousand pieces of glass against a wall. With one last thrust, the dam broke.

"Fuck, Haddie," I groaned her name like a prayer on my lips as I found my release. She followed suit seconds later, her body shuddering beneath mine as she cried out my name.

The room fell into silent tranquility but for our panting breaths and racing hearts that slowly dwindled down. She ran her fingers gently through my hair, anchoring me to reality after the post-orgasmic haze.

I held myself above her, not wanting to crush Haddie with my weight, but her arms around my back encouraged me to settle against her. Our bodies were slicked with sweat, heat radiating out from between us in the cool air of the room. Haddie gave a contented sigh beneath me, fingers tracing idle patterns on my back.

"God, that was..." she trailed off, words failing her. I chuckled, pressing a lazy kiss to the hollow of her throat.

"Yeah," I agreed, my voice muffled against her skin. "It was."

Silence fell over us again, comfortable and soothing. I felt Haddie's body relax beneath me as I listened to the steady rhythm of her heart matching mine. Her fingers brushed once along the shell of my ear before she pulled me slightly upward to look into her eyes again. Her gaze was soft yet filled with an intensity that took my breath away.

"I love you so much," she murmured quietly, a flicker of vulnerability showing in her eyes before being replaced by determined certainty.

"I love you too, Haddie," I replied huskily. "And our baby." My hand caressed her stomach, which was finally looking rounder and making it more real. Haddie finally saw a doctor, and it was a relief to find out everything was okay.

"Sometimes I can't believe this is all real," she whispered, kissing my chest. "Us finding each other like we did."

"No doubt in my mind you were meant for me," I replied, holding her tighter. "Sometimes a road takes you where you need to be, and you stop questioning how you got there. We're just supposed to enjoy the ride together."

32

One Month Later.

This is really happening and I'm about to marry Kaven. I'm the happiest woman in the world right now. "There, Hadleigh," Mom said, tugging at the waist of my wedding dress. "Thankfully, you're a thin girl, and your pregnancy isn't that noticeable with these pleats down the front."

"I have to say, Hadleigh, you're glowing, and I envy you finding your true love," Lizzie said from where she sat on the windowsill, careful not to wrinkle her bridesmaid dress.

"It will happen for you too," I assured her. "Just don't settle for less, no matter what happens."

She gave a soft laugh. "I doubt that. I'm hearing Grandfather is now using me for an alliance in the Flavio organization, and not with

Samuel."

"Stand your ground, Lizzie," I said right before Grandfather walked into the room, looking handsome in his tuxedo and all smiles. Kaven had confided in me the relationship between his mother and my grandfather; now I understand why this wedding is going forward, not just for me but for him. It explains a lot. I've never seen him so relaxed and happy.

"We're ready to begin," Grandfather said, taking my hand. "You look beautiful, Hadleigh, and whether you believe it or not, I only want to see you happy."

"I believe you," I replied, taking his hand and letting him lead me out of the room.

As we stepped into the corridor, the soft strains of the wedding march reached my ears. My heart pounded with a mix of excitement and nerves. Grandfather gave my hand a gentle squeeze, a silent reassurance.

The doors to the ballroom opened, and all eyes turned towards us. The room was a blur of familiar faces and flowers, but my focus was solely on Kaven standing at the altar, his eyes locked onto mine. He looked incredibly handsome in his tailored suit, his expression a mixture of love and awe.

With each step down the aisle, memories of our journey together flashed through my mind. The laughter, the tears, the promises whispered in the dark. This was our moment, the culmination of everything we had been through.

As I reached the altar, Kaven took my hand from Grandfather, his grip warm and steady. He leaned in slightly, whispering, "You're so damn beautiful."

"Thanks to you," I whispered back, feeling tears prick at the corners of my eyes.

The ceremony began, the words of the officiant a soothing background to the whirlwind of emotions swirling inside me. Kaven's eyes never left mine, and I felt an overwhelming surge of love and gratitude for this man who had become my everything.

When it was time for our vows, Kaven spoke first. His voice was steady but filled with emotion. "Haddie, from the moment I saw you standing by that waterfall, I knew my life would never be the same. You've shown me what it truly means to be in love to the core of my soul. I promise to love you, protect you, and cherish you for all the days of my life and never make you regret you chose me that night."

Tears streamed down my cheeks as I began my vows. "Kaven, you have become my everything, and my greatest love. With you, I've found my home. I promise to stand by you, to support you, and to love you fiercely and unconditionally, and I will never regret choosing you."

The officiant smiled warmly. "By the power vested in me, I now pronounce you husband and wife. You may kiss the bride."

Kaven pulled me close, his lips meeting mine in a kiss that was sweet and full of promise. The room erupted in applause, but all I could focus on was the man holding me, the man I would spend the rest of my life with.

As we turned to face our family and friends, I felt a profound sense of peace and happiness. This was our beginning, and I knew that whatever challenges lay ahead, we would face them together. With Kaven by my side, I was ready for anything.

The end for now, the story continues with Valley, and I have to tell you he's a tough one. Valley's handling of women is not like his friend Midnight. His story won't always be pretty and at times you're going to hate him, but hang in there. His demons are deep and to him very real and it takes losing Madeline to make him face them. The last book in this series is going to be one to remember.

Jarrod Warner, known as Valley to his club The Devil's House MC, is a man haunted by the shadows of his past, a ghost that literally won't let him move on. Working at the stripclub owned by The Devil's House MC, he unexpectedly reconnects with Madeline Wolfe aka 'Mandy' as she's known at the club, a dancer with a sweet nature that captivates him just as it did in high school. By day, Madeline is a dedicated dance instructor, supporting her disabled father and two-year-old daughter, and by night, she dances to make ends meet.

Jarrod's demons keep him from forming deep connections, yet Madeline finds a way to his heart no matter how hard he tried fighting her. Despite his desire to be with her, he pushes her away, leaving her heartbroken. Madeline, scarred by past hurts, refuses to endure more pain and protects herself from further heartbreak pushing forward, vowing to forget Jarrod, who treated her so horribly.

As Jarrod battles the past that haunts him and Madeline grapples with her feelings, an unseen threat looms over them. Someone is determined to stop and destroy the bond that is growing between the two, despite them trying to fight it and threatening to tear them apart forever.

Want to know more about Hope, Samuel, and the kidnapping that happened in Midnight's story? Then go to Kindle Vella where the story unfolded and the final version will be released on Kindle and paperback this fall.

Stay tuned for the South Carolina Series to begin. I feel the need for a change to get my creative juices flowing, so expect the stories to be grittier and darker. The first book will be Bolt's Flame.

* * *

* * *

* * *

Mhairi O'Reilly lives in Upstate, South Carolina. A native of West Virginia, Mhairi loves to read, Devoting many hours of her life to it. She always dreamed of writing her own stories; when the time arrived that she had the time, she jumped into it, not looking back.